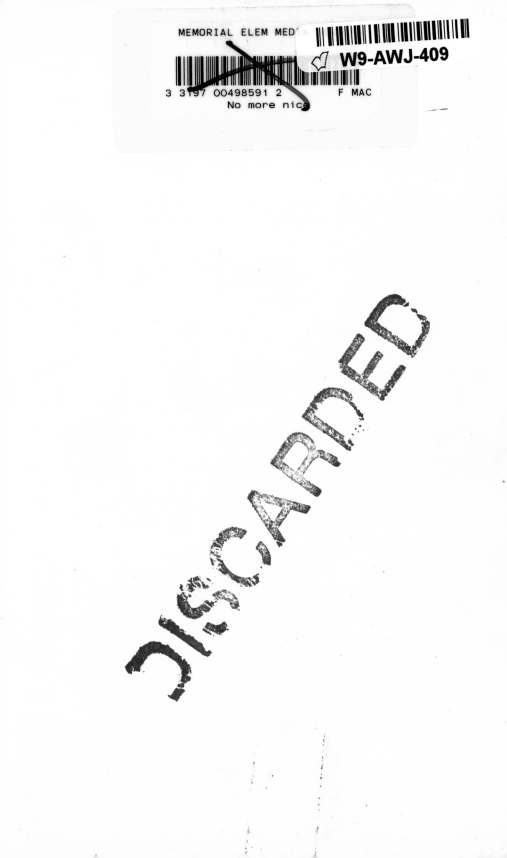

No More Nice

by Amy MacDonald

illustrated by Cat Bowman Smith

ORCHARD BOOKS
New York

Orchard Books
95 Madison Avenue
New York, NY 10016

Library of Congress Cataloging-in-Publication Data

MacDonald, Amy.
    No more nice / by Amy MacDonald ; illustrated by Cat Bowman
    Smith.
      p.   cm.
    "A Melanie Kroupa book"—Half t.p.
    Summary: Eleven-year-old Simon has been raised to be
  extremely well-behaved, but when he goes to visit his
  unconventional great-aunt he discovers that not everyone has
  the same ideas about good manners.
    ISBN 0-531-09542-8. — ISBN 0-531-08892-8
    [1. Behavior—Fiction.   2. Great-aunts—Fiction.
  3. Individuality—Fiction.]   I. Smith, Cat Bowman, ill.   II. Title.
  PZ7.M1463No   1996
  [Fic]—dc20   96-7661

Manufactured in the United States of America
Book design by Chris Hammill Paul

10 9 8 7 6 5 4 3 2 1

The text of this book is set in 12 point New Aster.
The illustrations are pen-and-ink.

For Mary Wright MacDonald

Sort of . . . You Know

Where was Aunt Matilda?

Simon Maxwell stepped off the train and scanned the empty station parking lot. I must be late, he thought nervously. She must have gotten tired of waiting and gone home.

And though he'd never met his great-aunt, he imagined how cross she would look—her bony hands twitching, her black eyes flashing—as Simon apologized for making her drive to the station twice.

"I'm very sorry, Aunt Matilda," he would say, even though it wasn't his fault that the train was late.

And then she'd say, grumpily, "Humph, well, nothing to be done about it. What's done is done."

The reason Simon was not looking forward to meeting his great-aunt Matilda was that he knew very little about her. And the few things he did know about her had him worried. He knew she was very old. And he knew that the older people got, the grouchier and crankier they got, and the less they liked children. And Aunt Matilda hadn't even wanted him to come and stay in the first place—that much he knew for sure. Simon had been told all his life that it was rude to invite yourself to someone else's house—but that's exactly what his parents had done. They'd called up Aunt Matilda and "invited" Simon to go stay with her and Uncle Philbert. Some vacation this was going to be!

Simon dragged his suitcase over to a bench and sat down. He watched a spider trapping a fly in its web while he tried to think what he might do if no one at all came to pick him up. This pleasant daydream was interrupted by the scrape of tires on gravel.

An ancient black car pulled into the station in a cloud of dust. The door opened and a woman heaved herself out. She had piles of white hair that seemed intent on es-

caping from the weight of an enormous hat with purple feathers. Her eyes drooped at the corners and were not black (as he had imagined) but emerald. And she was not tall and bony, but small, rounded, and padded like a comfortable armchair.

"You're Simon," she said, puffing, "and I'm late." Simon stuck out his hand politely, but the woman surrounded him in a hug that smelled of lavender and licorice. "So, Simon Maxwell," she said, releasing him halfway, "how does your corporosity seem to gashiate?"

"Excuse me?" said Simon.

"Your corporosity," said the woman. "Is it gashiating nicely?"

Since Simon couldn't answer this curious question, he asked meekly, "Are you Aunt Matilda?"

"Of course I am, child!" she said. "I did not introduce myself because it's much more fun to try to guess who everybody is. And please call me Mattie. Everyone does. Have you been waiting long?"

Simon hesitated. He couldn't lie. But if he told the truth, it might sound rude, as if he was cross at Aunt Matilda—Aunt Mattie—for being so late.

"Only twenty minutes," he said at last, struggling as usual to be both truthful and polite.

"Oh, good," said Aunt Mattie. "I always try to be at least fifteen minutes late."

If Simon was surprised at this remark, he didn't have time to show it. His aunt swept him into the dilapidated car, first removing a large goldfish bowl from the front seat. Water sloshed over the sides, and the startled fish swam in frantic circles. "Don't you just *hate* goldfish?" She sighed. Simon, who had two goldfish of his own for pets, kept silent. "Someone gave these to me and so I do my best to make their lives interesting. They must get so *bored* in that bowl. Same old view, day after day. I'm taking them for a drive today. A change of scenery will cheer them up, don't you agree?"

The car finally started on the third try, and they lurched from the parking lot. Simon buckled his seat belt and looked over at his great-aunt curiously. This wasn't easy to do, since a potted ivy plant hung from the roof of the car, swaying between them. Simon wanted to tell Aunt Mattie he agreed with her about goldfish. But he felt somehow that would be unfair to his other aunt, Aunt Bea, who had given the fish to him for his birthday. After all, goldfish were better than no pets at all, sort of. And Simon's mother had never allowed him to have other pets, because, she said, they made too much mess, and think of the fleas and the germs, and Simon would never take care of them, and who would look after them

when the family went on trips, and, and, and . . . Well, she had a million reasons.

But instead of explaining any of this to his great-aunt, Simon simply said, "Yes, Aunt Mattie."

He gripped the door handle as the car careened over the road at a terrific speed. His aunt, though broad, was quite short, and her head just barely peeped above the steering wheel. It was hard to imagine that she could see over it at all.

"Now then," she said briskly, "tell me truly, do I look the way you thought I would? Hmm? Be honest."

But Simon couldn't. He just couldn't find a polite way to say, "You're fatter than I imagined." Or maybe, "I thought you would be skinny, like a witch." Or, "You are even older than I thought." If there was one thing his parents had taught him, it was that it was rude to make "personal" comments about people. You mustn't say they were fat or thin or had dimples or didn't have dimples or were hairy or bald or anything—even if it was true.

Grown-ups, he had noticed, always seemed to feel that it was perfectly okay for *them* to make personal comments about children. Most of his parents' friends greeted Simon with the same remark: "My, how tall you are." Yes, it was true, Simon was taller than most boys in fifth grade, but hearing it said out loud so much always made him feel bashful.

And once they'd finished commenting on his height, they'd always say, "And look at that great hair! Where'd you get those curls?" (Simon was often tempted to answer that he'd sent away for them from the back of a cereal box. But of course he never did.) Then they always added, "Why do boys get all the curls?"

Simon would stare at the ground, blushing and waiting for the freckle comment. "Well, say, did you ever see so many freckles in your life?" they'd ask, as if they were the first person to notice them. Then they'd make the freckle joke. "Bet you could play connect the dots with those freckles! Ha-ha-ha!"

The more Simon thought about Aunt Mattie, the more amazed—and grateful—he was that she hadn't made a single one of the tall/curly hair/freckle remarks. Instead, she had asked him what *he* thought of *her*.

"Well," said Simon slowly. "I thought you'd be . . ."

"Taller? Thinner?" asked Aunt Mattie. And she laughed—a little bit like geese honking in a snowstorm, he decided. Nothing at all like the genteel titter that was his mother's laugh, or the polite smile that his father often wore, or Aunt Bea's loud bray. Watching her, Simon was upset to see that she closed her eyes each time she laughed. The car wobbled onto the edge of the road and then back again. Simon closed his eyes, too.

How does she manage to read my mind like that? he wondered. Maybe she *is* a witch.

That would explain why no one in his house ever mentioned her name. And why, when his mother had had to find somewhere for Simon to stay during spring vacation, the last person she'd thought of was his great-aunt Matilda.

"Aunt Matilda?" Uncle Fred had asked in surprise. "*My* aunt Matilda?"

"Yes," Mrs. Maxwell had said. "She's George's aunt, too." George was Simon's father, who was in Japan on a business trip just then.

Uncle Fred had raised his eyebrows just a tiny bit, which meant he didn't approve. "Isn't she sort of . . . *you know?*"

"Is she?" Mrs. Maxwell had said. "I've never actually met her. But I just don't have any choice. No one else can take him while you're staying here."

So it was decided: during spring vacation, Simon would go to stay with his great-aunt in the country. That way, Aunt Bea and Uncle Fred could move into the Maxwells' only guest room. And their son, the loathsome cousin Parker, would have Simon's room. And Simon smiled and was brave about it, even though he didn't want Parker in his room. Even though he didn't want to go away. Even though he'd never met Great-aunt Matilda. And even though she was a bit *"you know."*

Simon had worried for weeks about what *"you know"* could mean. Did it mean she was nasty—a coldhearted child-hater? Or horribly strict? Or perhaps extremely old and fussy? Now that the dreadful day had come, he glanced over at his great-aunt. He could be wrong, but she didn't seem coldhearted, or cranky. Or fussy.

Was she a witch, then? Is that what *"you know"* meant?

Too Much Bother

Simon's thoughts were interrupted as the car drove into a dirt driveway and came to a halt in a hail of flying gravel outside a ramshackle red farmhouse.

A row of very tall, very bright salmon-colored flowers drooped by the front door. A swaybacked old white horse stood on the porch, calmly eating daffodils out of the window box. Two brilliant green peacocks perched on the chimney. Against the front porch leaned an old motorcycle that someone had taken apart and never put back together. And beside that was an amazingly ugly carved wooden bed. From the paddock by the barn, a trio of camels stared suspiciously at Aunt Mattie and Simon as they got out of the car.

Inside, the house was even stranger. An enormous rubber-tree plant grew up one wall and across the length of the ceiling, suspended by threads. Stacked everywhere were books and magazines and junk. There were tennis rackets with no strings, skis with no bindings, and golf clubs with no heads. Most startling were the cats—at least a dozen of them draped about here and there like cast-off clothing.

"Please, please, don't get up," said Aunt Mattie to the cats at large. She flung her hat onto a table and collapsed onto the only piece of furniture in sight, a huge lumpy sofa. "Confusticate these cats!" she exclaimed as several that she had sat on protested loudly, wriggling out from under her bulk. A small cloud of cat hair was released into the air, and Simon noticed that the couch was thick with it. Imagine the dirt, he thought. Imagine the mess. Imagine the fleas.

Aunt Mattie turned to Simon. "Now, then, young Simon. Here you are in the country. I'm sorry you can't meet Uncle Philbert until tomorrow—he's off visiting a sick relative. But your wish is my command. What would you like to do?"

Simon looked at his feet and mumbled. "I don't know—whatever you like. I don't want to be any bother."

"Bother!" snorted Mattie. "Bother is what I like best. People who are no bother are like . . . like *furniture*. Furniture is absolutely no bother at all. That's why I have so little of it. Cats, on the other hand, are nothing *but* bother. The same with plants. Always needing something: a bit of water or fertilizer, a pruning—I'm talking about the plants, not the cats—or to be let in, or to be let out, or to be fed, or petted, or brushed—the cats, that is, not the plants."

There was a long pause.

Mattie glanced at her grandfather clock, whose hands stood at nine o'clock.

"Goodness, it's . . . it's . . ." She grabbed a pencil and

wrote some figures on an old envelope. "And carry the eleven makes ... It's quarter past twelve. Snack time. Come and talk to me while I make it. Then we'll go out and meet the animals."

Simon followed his great-aunt silently into the kitchen, where a pair of cats were sleeping in the warming oven of a vast iron cookstove. The stove gave off a delicious warmth. A smell of fresh baking filled the air.

"You look confused, Simon," said Mattie. "Don't you want a snack?"

"In our house," Simon said in a voice that was hardly louder than a whisper, "snack time is at ten-thirty, and twelve o'clock is lunchtime."

"Shut your mutt!"

Instead, Simon let his mouth sag wide open.

"What?" he asked in a whisper.

"Say please!" came the peevish order again. But this time, Simon could see that it didn't come from his aunt, but from a gray parrot that was clinging upside down to an overhead lamp.

"Oh, really, Runcible." Mattie sighed. "You are a contumelious creature. Is that any way to greet my long-lost nephew?" The parrot stopped combing her feathers with her beak and looked at Mattie.

"Stuff it," said the bird, adding for good measure, "dog breath."

Mattie shook her head. "She's quite incorrigible," she said as she put a kettle onto the cookstove to boil. "It's best to ignore her."

"Now, about the question of snack time: in this house, it's snack time whenever we decide to have a snack. Let's see what we have here."

10

She went over to a row of crockery jars on the counter and began opening them. The one marked FLOUR contained bright red pistachio nuts. The one marked SUGAR contained black licorice sticks. The one marked COFFEE contained a heap of chunky cookies. Mattie sniffed them.

"Butterscotch-peppermint cookies," she said, "I

think. Or perhaps they're chocolate-raspberry. Might have to try one to be sure." She took a large bite. "Butterscotch-raspberry without a doubt," she said, with her mouth full of cookie. "What would you like?"

"I don't mind," said Simon. So Mattie filled a plate with pistachio nuts and butterscotch-raspberry cookies and went to the cupboard.

"Now for tea," she said.

Simon, trying hard to be polite, said, "I'm not allowed to drink tea."

"I'm glad to hear it," said Mattie. "Why would anyone want to? It's a filthy drink made from ground-up leaves, for goodness sake. I don't drink it, either. Same with coffee—dried beans soaked in warm water! Yuck! *And* it turns your teeth brown." She shuddered. "Sometimes it amazes me what otherwise-normal human beings will eat or drink."

Simon smiled, and Mattie kept going.

"Consider wine," she said as she put out mugs and took the kettle off the stove. "Wine is made from rotten grapes. Rotten grapes! Did you ever taste it?"

"Once," said Simon, making a face.

"Exactly," said Mattie. "Now then, for tea I'm afraid we don't have any of the ground-up leaves, but we do have"—she read the labels of some jars—"ginger tea, raspberry tea, cinnamon tea, or peach tea."

Simon started to say, "I don't mind" again, then stopped. "Ginger sounds interesting," he said.

"That's the spirit. How do you take your tea? Milk? Sugar? Ice cream?"

"Just plain, please," Simon murmured.

She poured them both out steaming mugs, adding a

dollop of vanilla ice cream to hers. Simon simply gaped, until he remembered that it was not polite to stare.

"*Say thank you!*"

"Thank you," said Simon automatically. Then he realized it had been Runcible, the parrot, speaking, not Aunt Mattie, and he blushed.

"Now then," said Aunt Mattie, taking a gulp of ginger tea. "Tell me, how are your parents?"

"They're fine," said Simon rapidly, thinking of his father, who was never home, and when he was home never had time for anything but sleeping. He began to apologize for his parents. "Mother and Father wish they could have driven me, but Father's boss called at the last minute and said he had to go on a business trip. And Mother had to stay to help Aunt Bea unpack her things and—"

But Aunt Mattie simply laughed at this apology, as if it were the most natural thing in the world for parents to have put their young son on a train to visit a great-aunt he'd never met.

"Your father came to stay with me once. But I haven't seen him since he was ten years old. How old are you now, Simon?"

"I'll be eleven in two weeks, after vacation." Simon knew that it was polite for Mattie to ask him how old *he* was. But it would be rude for him to ask her how old *she* was—yet another grown-up rule he didn't understand. So he kept quiet. To his surprise, she volunteered the information.

"I'm seventy-two," she said. "And a half."

"That's nice," said Simon, thinking it was incredibly old.

"Now tell me about yourself, Simon. How do you like school? I assume you go to some sort of school?"

"It's very nice, thank you," said the boy, looking into his mug and thinking of the long gray building he went to every day.

"And your teacher, do you like her?"

"Yes," said Simon without looking up. He was thinking of Mrs. Biggs. Mrs. Biggs was rude to all the boys—and even some of the girls—in his class. All but him. She was never rude to Simon because Simon was always quiet and well behaved. He never talked without raising his hand first. He always knew the right answer. Mrs. Biggs loved Simon.

"And do you have lots of friends?"

"Oh yes," said Simon quickly. "Lots and lots."

"I see," said Aunt Mattie softly. Then she added, "Simon, you're not drinking your tea. Don't you like it?"

"Oh yes," Simon said. "It's very nice, thank you." He took a little sip. It was scalding and burned his lip. He gasped.

"Dear me, it's too hot," said Aunt Mattie. "That's why I always put ice cream in. I'm sorry. Did you hurt yourself?"

"Not at all," said Simon, blinking back tears of pain. "It's just right." And to prove it to her, he took another sip, and burned his lip again. "Just fine, thank you."

Aunt Mattie gave him a long look.

"You Maxwell boys," she said to herself, "you're all the same. I can see I have lots of work to do." And to Simon's deep and lasting astonishment, she leaned back in her seat, put her handkerchief to her mouth, and burped loudly.

14

After Aunt Mattie burped—or "belched," as his mother would have called it—Simon was so shocked that he hardly noticed what happened next.

Aunt Mattie jabbed her thumb into her forehead, looked at Simon, and then reached over and punched him lightly on the shoulder.

"There," she said happily. "That's what we do in this house when someone burps."

"What?" asked Simon. "You what?"

"If someone burps," said Mattie cheerily, "everyone has to stick their thumb to their forehead. The last person in the room to do it gets punched." Simon started to smile and Mattie looked very pleased. "What do you do in *your* house?"

"In our house," said Simon, and he stopped smiling, "if you burp—I mean, belch—you get sent to your room."

"Goodness!" exclaimed Mattie. "Even your parents? How interesting."

"Of course not," said Simon. "My parents never get sent to their room."

"Even when they burp? That's not fair."

"My parents never belch," explained Simon.

"They don't?"

"No. It's very rude, you know. Oh, I'm sorry, I didn't mean that you—"

"Not at all," said Mattie happily. "What you say is most interesting. Who says it's rude to burp?"

"Well, my parents, and, well—everyone does."

"Everyone? Did you know that in many countries it is considered *polite* to belch after a meal?"

"No!" Simon was shocked.

"Yes, in Germany, for example, it is a sign that you enjoyed your meal. It is a compliment to the cook. And, Simon?"

"Yes?"

"In this house, it is considered polite to burp. Okay?"

Simon smiled. "Okay," he said.

Mattie laughed. Goose honks on a snowy day, thought Simon. Definitely.

So Many Questions

"Come along Simon. I'll introduce you to the llamas. You'll like them. They're extremely nasty."

Simon trotted obediently behind Aunt Mattie. He was full of questions, simply bursting. He couldn't help wishing that it wasn't bad manners to pepper someone with questions, the way Aunt Mattie had peppered him. He wanted to know why Aunt Mattie always liked to be fifteen minutes late, where she sat when the sofa was full, how the peacocks got on the roof, why her tennis rackets had no strings, whether she really was a witch.

But he kept his mouth shut, as he had been taught.

"Why so silent, Simon?"

"Well, Mother says never to speak until spoken to. And Father says it's rude to ask too many questions."

Mattie turned, her hands on her wide hips. She opened her mouth to say something, then closed it again. After a bit, she said simply, "Your father appears to have forgotten everything I ever taught him. I think it's rude *not* to ask questions. Seems like you're not interested."

"Oh, but—"

"Take my sofa, for instance—never asks any questions at all, and I think that's because it finds me boring. Am I boring you, Simon?"

Simon smiled, and ran to keep up with her. He couldn't remember when he had felt *less* bored. "No, Aunt Mattie."

"The *sofa*," continued Aunt Mattie, striding off as if she hadn't heard him, "the sofa never speaks until spoken to. Have you ever stopped to think, young Simon, what the world would be like if *no one* ever spoke until spoken to? Hmm?"

"Well—"

"It would be an awfully quiet place, Simon. And it would make using the phone difficult, now wouldn't it?"

Simon tried to imagine a phone conversation in which no one was allowed to talk first. He smiled. Then Mattie started giggling—there was no other word for it—and Simon felt himself starting to laugh. It was a small laugh, but it grew and grew until his sides ached, and he had to wrap his arms around his ribs and sit down. Aunt Mattie, meanwhile, was gasping for breath, and pretty soon she had to sit down, too.

After they had caught their breath, Mattie looked at Simon, but he remained silent. At last she said, "What else do your parents say?"

"What?"

" 'Don't speak till spoken to.' 'Don't ask questions.' I'll bet they also say, 'Children should be seen and not heard.' Am I right?"

Simon shook his head. She *was* a witch! "How did you know?"

"And probably: 'Don't speak with your mouth full' and 'Don't eat with your mouth open.' Or is it: 'Don't eat with your mouth full' and 'Don't speak with your mouth open'?"

Simon smiled at the thought of trying to speak without opening his mouth. Or eating only when his mouth was empty.

"And then at mealtime they tell you to sit down, and once you sit down, they tell you to sit *up*. Which is it—up or down?"

"You seem to know a lot about our house," said Simon.

"Well," said Mattie solemnly, "I know a lot about Maxwells. And I know a lot about grown-ups." She struggled to her feet. "Let's go find those llamas. They don't have any silly rules. In fact, they are the rudest creatures on God's earth."

What Simon had taken for camels were in fact long-haired brown-and-white llamas. They were named Mr. Rude, Mr. Crude, and Mr. Ugly. All three crowded over to inspect him when Mattie was filling their feed troughs. As Simon watched, the biggest llama, Mr. Ugly, curled back his lips and spat at him. A big gob of llama spittle struck Simon in the middle of his neat button-down white shirt. Simon yelped.

"Disgusting dromedaries!" shouted Mattie, shaking her fist at them. "Flocculent, flea-bitten varmints! Why," she said to Simon, "they'd as soon spit at you as look at you. They're utterly good-for-nothing."

Simon, starting to smile, looked down at the brown stain on his shirt and thought of what his mother would say about it. His smile vanished.

Aunt Mattie seemed, as usual, to be reading his thoughts.

"Back at the house," she said, "I have a bottle of Sure-fire Llama Spit Stain Remover. Your poor shirt! It's entirely my fault, dearie. I should never have brought you out here in your best Sunday going-to-meeting clothes. Let's go in and change."

"Into what?"

"Why, into some work clothes."

"But I don't have any."

Mattie surveyed his spotless gray school pants, his shiny leather shoes, his neatly pressed shirt, his blue blazer (he'd taken the tie off in the train and stuffed it in his pocket).

"What's in that suitcase, then? No blue jeans?"

"No."

"No T-shirts?"

"No."

"No sneakers?"

"No. My mother packed for me, and she insisted that I bring lots of nice clothes. All I've got is school clothes like this."

"Well." Her hands perched on her hips in disbelief. "We'll have to do something about that. But for now, I'll take you to meet the horses."

First was the old white nag that had been on the porch.

"That's Sugar," said Mattie. "And she's even older than I am. In horse years, of course. Imagine that." Sugar put out her head for the sugar cube that Mattie had brought in her pocket. Simon, who'd always been told that horses bite, touched her muzzle cautiously. He was trying to work up his courage to ask about riding her when another horse cantered up. This was a shaggy young chestnut, and he shook his head and danced nervously around Mattie while she held out a carrot for him. Simon thought him the most beautiful horse he'd ever seen.

"His name is Hero, and he's a love," said Mattie. "He's mad about carrots."

"Can I ride him?" asked Simon, forgetting his manners

in his excitement. He added hastily, "That is, if it's not too much trouble for you."

"I'm sorry, dear," said his aunt. "You can't ride him. No one can. You see, the man who owned him before me was a beast. He was vicious to Hero. One day, Hero decided he'd had enough, and he bucked that man off. Nearly killed him. And from that day on, Hero wouldn't let anyone on his back. He was on his way to the glue factory when I bought him. And the longer it's been since a horse has been ridden, the wilder he is."

"Why did you buy a horse that no one can ride?"

"Because I admired him so much. He stood up for himself, even though it almost cost him his life. That's why I named him Hero."

"What about Sugar?"

"She's too old to be ridden. I got her at the glue factory, too. You see, I'm too old to be ridden, too. Oh, you know what I mean—too old to be any use to anyone. And I kept wondering what it would be like if someone sent *me* to the glue factory."

"Why do you have llamas if they're 'good-for-nothing'?"

"Because they don't take any guff from anyone."

"What do you mean?"

"They won't let anyone else push them around. I like that in an animal. You notice I don't have any 'useful' animals like sheep or cows or chickens. They're such goody-goodies. Just sit there doing what they're told. They make wool. They give milk. They lay eggs. So dull! I like animals who are rude and don't cooperate—animals that are lots of bother and no earthly use to anyone. Like cats. Or peacocks. They spend all day looking at themselves in the mirror. Why, just try asking *peacocks* to lay eggs or do something useful!"

"Or the parrot," said Simon. "She'd probably insult you!"

"Absolutely," said Mattie. "That's why I'm so fond of her. She's like Hero, no use to anyone. The pet-store owner couldn't sell her, because of her foul mouth. And he couldn't keep her in the store anymore because she was driving away customers. One day, a woman came in and asked what she could do about her macaw—that's a large bird—who was feeling poorly. And just as the owner opened his mouth, Runcible said, 'Stuff it!' Just like that."

Mattie emitted some loud honks of laughter. "The lady turned on her heel and stormed out of the pet store. And Runcible yelled after her, 'Put a sock in it!' Why, the poor store owner practically *paid* me to take Runcible away."

Simon laughed, remembering the shock he'd felt when Runcible first insulted him in the kitchen. "And why do you always—"

Mattie raised her eyebrows. "My goodness, but you're suddenly full of questions."

"I—I'm sorry," stammered Simon. "It's just—you said you liked ques—"

"The more the better. Carry on. You may speak without being spoken to."

"Well, I was going to ask you why you always try to be fifteen minutes late. I thought it was rude to be late." Then he blushed, thinking that what he had just said sounded extremely rude.

To his surprise Mattie laughed. "Yes, terribly," she

agreed. "But so much more exciting that way, don't you think? What did you do while you were waiting at the station for me?"

"Well, I watched a spider catching a fly. She wrapped it up as tight as she could in her—"

"You see!" interrupted Aunt Mattie. That was another thing about Aunt Mattie. She interrupted all the time. She seemed not to know that was bad manners. "Now, if I'd arrived on time," she said, "you would have missed the spider and the fly! Thank heavens I remembered to forget."

"Forget what?" asked Simon.

"The time your train arrived, silly. Anything else you want to know?"

"Yes," said Simon. "Why is your furniture outdoors, in the yard? Won't that bed get ruined?"

"Oh, yes. I hope so. It's like leftovers."

"Leftovers?"

"Yes. You know, when you have a little of something left over from a meal, not enough to eat, but you can't quite bear to throw it out. So you put it in a container at the back of the fridge for a month or so until it goes all green and moldy. Then you open it up and say, '*Yuck!*' And *then* you can throw it out."

"You *want* to throw out your furniture?"

"Oh yes. I've told you: furniture is boring. That bed was given to me by *my* great-aunt. It's some sort of antique, you see, a family heirloom. So I couldn't just take it to the dump. And nobody in their right mind would actually buy it, it's so ugly. So I'm euthanizing it first."

"What's that?"

"It means to put something out of its misery—like

when you have a very old, sick pet put to sleep. I had to do that to a plant once, too."

"You put a plant out of its misery?"

"Yes. A cactus. Someone gave it to me—why I can't imagine. Oh, it was the most boring, miserable plant in the world. Never grew, never blossomed. Never did anything. Just sat there looking like a pincushion. Of course I overwatered it. I kept thinking if I gave it some more water, something might actually happen. Well, to make a long story short, one winter night I put it out on the porch and put it out of its misery. It was a quick and painless death.

"Now, what else would you like to know? Don't be shy."

"Well . . . why do you have tennis rackets without any strings?"

"Because they're for people who are only a little bit interested in playing tennis," replied Aunt Mattie, looking stern. "You know the kind: they come to visit and you say, 'Would you like to play tennis?' and they say, 'Well, sure, I guess,' and so you get out the rackets and they look at them and say, 'Oh gosh, that's too bad,' and it saves them the trouble of having to do something they really don't like. The same with those golf clubs."

"I see," said Simon, who didn't.

Sometimes talking to Aunt Mattie made him feel dizzy.

That night, as Aunt Mattie was tucking him in, she said, "Uncle Philbert will be home later tonight. He's a terrible curmudgeon, but I'm going to ask him to give you lessons."

Simon's heart sank. He didn't know what a curmudgeon was, but it didn't sound great. "That's very kind of you, Aunt Mattie," he said. "But really, I'm taking piano and French lessons already at—"

"Not French lessons, silly," said his aunt.

"Then what are they?"

"Let's just say they're called . . . well, un-lessons."

"What are—"

"Tomorrow," said his aunt. "You'll see."

How Do You Do?

Next morning, Simon lay in bed, not quite awake, and thought, as one does, that he was at home. Any moment he would be awakened by his mother's knock and her cheerful morning greeting: "Rise and shine." She would come into his room with an armful of freshly ironed shirts and pants for school, pull the curtains, and give him a peck on the cheek.

Instead, what happened was, Simon started to choke. This may have had something to do with Raspberry, a large, warm, ginger-colored cat who had climbed onto his pillow, settled comfortably on Simon's head, and placed his tail in Simon's mouth. When Simon objected to this, dislodging Raspberry as gently as possible, the cat shot him a look as if to say, *Really! How rude!* Then he settled onto Simon's chest, put his nose up against Simon's nose, and purred loudly.

Simon lay there, stroking Raspberry and wondering what it was about waking up in a strange bed that could make you feel so suddenly homesick. Probably just that everything seemed so different. Not bad. Just different.

He thought back to last night's amazing dinner. It had started off with a large slice of lemon meringue pie. "No vegetables or chicken for you, young man, until you've finished your pie," Aunt Mattie had said sternly as she set it before him. Needless to say, he ate the whole piece. And then when she produced the chicken and peas and potatoes, she hadn't minded a bit when he hadn't finished his peas.

As Simon lay there, delicious smells began wafting up from the kitchen. The last thing his mother had said to him was, "Don't wake Aunt Matilda and Uncle Philbert up in the mornings. Old people like to sleep late. Wait till she wakes you."

But she might never come to wake him. And the smells coming from the kitchen proved she was already awake. So Simon finally decided to go downstairs. Just as he walked into the kitchen, his great-aunt opened one of the many doors in the cookstove and removed a large pizza. It was bubbling hot. She dislodged a cat from one of the warming ovens and replaced it with the pizza.

"Homemade," said Mattie proudly. "Sit right down and I'll cut you a slice. Now then, how does your corporosity seem to gashiate today?"

Once again, Simon was speechless. "Pizza for breakfast?" he asked finally.

"And fruit salad," said his aunt, serving him a generous triangle of gooey pizza, along with a bowl of sliced oranges, pineapples, and bananas. "Something wrong?"

"Oh, no, no, not at all. It's just . . . well . . . I don't usually . . ."

28

"Have pizza for breakfast?"

"No."

"Why on earth not?"

"I guess it's not good for you."

"What *do* you usually have for breakfast?"

"Oh, I have the same thing every morning: Super Frosted Rice Poppies with marshmallows."

"And *that's* good for you?"

"Well, it is kinda sugary—"

"Do you ever have pizza for dinner or lunch?"

"Yes."

"And *then* it's good for you? But in the morning it's not?"

"Well, I—"

"It is just a question of what you are used to, isn't it? Did you know that in England they have smoked fish for breakfast, and sometimes kidneys?"

"Disgusting!"

"And other countries have goat cheese for breakfast."

"Gross!"

"The Japanese have rice for breakfast."

"Yuck!"

" 'Yuck'? What do you think Rice Poppies are made of?"

"I . . . well, rice, I guess, but—"

"And another thing. What would you say to your mother if she gave you the same thing for lunch every single day of your life?"

"I would get really bored of it and ask for something else."

"But you can eat the same thing every morning for breakfast—cereal and orange juice—and never get bored?"

"Gee, I never thought of it like that."

"Maybe you should try it, hmm?"

Simon looked at his pizza. Suddenly, it looked very tasty.

He was spared from having to answer Aunt Mattie by the banging of the screen door. A man in faded overalls and a plaid shirt entered the kitchen, pulled out a chair, and sat down.

"You're late," said Mattie.

"Good," said the man gruffly. "I do my best." He had longish silvery hair, a droopy white mustache, and appeared about the same age as Mattie. Unlike Mattie, however, he was long and lean as a garden rake. He turned to Simon for the first time, and Simon felt a little scared. Uncle Philbert—he assumed this man must be Uncle Philbert—reminded him of the extremely grouchy grandfather in the book *Heidi*. Simon had an uncomfortable feeling that he was about to find out just exactly what the word *curmudgeon* meant. He took a deep breath and addressed his great-uncle as he had been taught to do.

"How do you do?" said Simon politely.

"What?" asked the man.

"I said, 'How do you do?' " repeated Simon loudly.

"No need to shout," said the man. "I'm not deaf. I heard you very well the first time. And I answered you: 'What?' "

"Excuse me?" asked Simon.

"How do I do *what*?" said the man grumpily. "How do I do crossword puzzles? How do I do my laundry? How do I do long division? Different answer for each question, isn't there?"

Simon had once read a book about a girl named Alice who went down a rabbit hole and met a large caterpillar that was very rude to her. Right now, he felt a lot like Alice.

"You'll be Simon," the man said between mouthfuls of pizza.

Suddenly, instead of feeling scared, Simon felt mad.

"I'll be Simon," he said slowly, "if you'll be Uncle Philbert."

To Simon's surprise, Philbert—for it was he—laughed so hard at this that awful things happened to the tablecloth. After Mattie had sponged up the table and wiped the tears from her own eyes, she turned to Uncle Philbert.

"That's one for Simon," she said happily.

"Humph!" snorted Philbert. "I thought you told me the kid was too polite for his own good."

"Well, he's a fast learner. All it took was ten minutes of being around the rudest man in the world. Now I will leave you two together while I feed the animals. You can get started right in on your un-lessons."

When Aunt Mattie got back from feeding the animals, Simon and Uncle Philbert were still sitting at the kitchen table. Uncle Philbert had his hand under his shirt, cupped under his armpit. He looked a little embarrassed when Mattie walked in.

"I was just starting him off with an un-lesson on Rude Noises," he explained. Then he added gruffly, "Can you believe this boy is nearly eleven years old and no one has ever taught him how to make armpit noises? What kind of an education you gettin' in them schools anyhow?

That's right, you just kind of put your hand there and squeeze. Good, excellent."

Simon giggled. He had just made a noise that sounded remarkably like Uncle Fred blowing his nose.

"Uncle Philbert, why are they called un-lessons?"

"Why, some of it's stuff you got to un-learn, you see? And others is just stuff that you can't be a real kid un-less'n you know how to do it. Now then, my boy, can you spit?"

Simon shook his head.

"Well, I'll be pickled. I really will. You poor neglected child. Come on outside and I'll show you."

Un-lessons

The next four or five days went by in a blur for Simon.

He got used to waking up with the cat Raspberry in his mouth. In fact, it soon got so he couldn't sleep without Raspberry purring gently on his head.

He got used to having strange food: pizza, macaroni, baked apples for breakfast; cake or pie for dinner, with vegetables for dessert. In fact, after several days of eating pie for dinner, he discovered that he sort of looked forward to the peas and carrots.

He got used to ginger tea served at all times of the day. In fact, he found it was totally delicious, especially with ice cream to cool it down.

He even learned the answer to the ritual morning question about how his "corporosity seemed to gashiate." The answer, apparently, was, "Very discombobulate, great congruity, dissimilarity." When Simon asked Philbert what this nonsense meant, Philbert answered, "Who knows? All I know is, it makes about as much sense as being asked how you 'do' and answering, 'Fine.' Tell me what *that* means!"

Uncle Philbert and Aunt Mattie seemed determined to fill in the gaps in Simon's appalling education. Each morning started with an un-lesson after breakfast. Within a day, Simon was making great armpit noises. He could even manage to "play tunes" like "Yankee Doodle."

Spitting, however, was harder, and Simon was practicing on the front porch the second morning when Philbert asked him if he'd brought his jackknife with him. "I want to teach you how to whittle," he explained.

"I don't have a knife," said Simon. Then, seeing Philbert's look of disbelief, he added, "My parents are afraid I might cut myself."

Uncle Philbert just nodded a few times. "You can borrow mine," he said at last. Simon reached for the beautiful bone-handled knife, enjoying the heft of it in his palm, and Philbert showed him how to unfold the blades safely. He handed him a stick of poplar. "Got to start with a soft wood. Now, always whittle away from yourself," he said, demonstrating with a few quick flicks that removed the bark. Simon whittled slowly and carefully, and pretty soon the poplar stick was smoothed out on all sides, shiny and white.

"What are we going to make with it?" asked Simon.

"Make?" said Philbert, looking shocked again. "You don't 'make' anything. You just whittle for the fun of whittlin'. To get it nice and smooth. Can't we do something purely for the heck of it?"

"Well, some people"—namely his father—"might say that was a waste of time," said Simon.

"That's exactly right," said Uncle Philbert. "It's a grand way to waste some time."

They both smiled and took turns whittling for a while. Then Philbert took the jackknife and showed Simon how to play a game called "mumblety-peg." You used the rounded hole-puncher blade and took turns with the knife, balancing the tip first on your finger, then on your

knee, then on your foot and all different parts of your body. The point was to toss it up in the air in such a way that the blade stuck straight into the ground when it landed. Each time it stuck in, you got another turn. As Simon managed an expert toss with his foot, he wondered what his mother would think if she could see him now.

Another day, Philbert showed Simon how to make an earsplitting whistle with two fingers in his mouth. For Simon, who had only just discovered how to whistle in the usual way, this was much harder to learn. He practiced everywhere he went for two days, making a circle with thumb and forefinger, placing them over his folded-back tongue, and blowing hard. Sometimes he nearly fainted from dizziness as he blew over and over. But nothing came out, not even a squeak. Then, suddenly, on the third day, an extraordinary sound came from his mouth. It was so loud, it startled him. He blew again. Another sharp whistle. It was the most piercing noise he had ever heard.

As he practiced, an even more surprising thing happened. Hero, who had been far out in the pasture, heard him and came trotting up to the fence. Simon laughed and reached timidly out to touch his head. "Now we have a secret signal, old pal," he said. And Hero shook his mane, as if agreeing.

A Warning

Finally, the day came when they could no longer put off buying Simon some work clothes.

Philbert said he'd rather die and go to purgatory than go clothes shopping, so he went outside to mow the lawn. But when Mattie and Simon went out to get in the car, they found Uncle Philbert glaring at the lawn mower. He had yanked on the handle to start the mower, and the handle had come right off in his hand.

"Confusticate this machine!" he shouted. "You misbegotten metal monster!" He aimed a kick at a rear wheel, which promptly fell off. "You, you son-of-a-tractor!"

Aunt Mattie gave him a knowing look and fetched him a pair of handheld shears. "Why don't you try these, dear? Even you can't break these."

But Uncle Philbert insisted on going into town with them to buy a new part for the lawn mower, so they all piled into the old car.

This time, Simon sat in back so Philbert could have the

passenger seat. The goldfish were still there, and Simon was instructed to "do something to cheer them up." The backseat, which was apparently seldom used to transport human beings, was heaped with library books, garden tools, jigsaw puzzles, blankets, and magazines with titles like *The Compleat Guide to Llama Care*. Mattie threw the car into reverse, and they lurched out of the driveway and onto the road. Once again, Simon found himself gripping the door handle to keep from falling off the seat. It was all he could do to hold the goldfish bowl upright.

"Awfully quiet in the backseat," sang out Aunt Mattie after several minutes. "Are we boring you?"

"No, Aunt Mattie," said Simon.

"Good. Then, let's play fifty questions."

"How do you play that?"

"Well, you ask fifty questions, and I answer them."

Simon laughed. "Okay. Why is it that you do all the driving? In most of the families I know, the father always drives."

"That's because—" Philbert started to say, but as usual, he was interrupted.

"I'm a much better driver than Philbert." Mattie laughed.

"Mendacious woman!" sputtered Philbert. He turned around to look at Simon. "The real reason is, Mattie has a magic way with machines. You take this car, for instance. It's a 1946 New York taxicab. It had two hundred thousand miles on it. Like just about everything else we own, it was on its way to the glue factory, or whatever it's called—"

"The scrap pile," suggested Mattie.

39

"But she bought it for fifty dollars. Then she got a few books on engine repair, took the whole thing apart, right there in our front yard. Put it all back together again, and this car has purred like a pastry for the last ten years."

"Philbert," said Mattie, pursing her lips, "pastry doesn't purr."

"Did Uncle Philbert help you repair the car?"

"Uncle Philbert!" said Mattie with an explosive laugh. "Why, if Bertie even gets within spitting distance of an engine—any kind of engine—it keels straight over and dies. They wilt like salted snails. The man has a curse on him."

"Sad but true," admitted Uncle Philbert, looking at the lawn mower handle.

"On the other hand," said Mattie, "he is wonderful with the animals. Even the llamas behave for him."

Gradually during this conversation, Simon had become aware of something strange going on behind him. He turned to peer out the back window. And gasped. A police car was following right behind them. And its blue lights were flashing. Simon knew what that meant: Trouble with a capital *T*. He looked at Mattie. She appeared not to have noticed anything amiss.

"Aunt Mattie," said Simon in a croaky voice, "there's a police car behind us."

"Yes, dear," said Mattie, and kept right on driving and chatting with Philbert.

Simon didn't know what to do next. His father had once gotten a speeding ticket, and Simon had hidden under the backseat during the whole awful thing. His father had grown red in the face and said terrible things under his breath as he pulled off the road. Then the policeman had sauntered over to their car, knocked on the driver's window, and demanded to see his father's license and registration. Simon, lying on the floor, felt overcome with shame and embarrassment. He had never been sent to the principal's office and made to sit in the red chair in the hall so that everyone walking by would know he had been bad. But this must be exactly what it felt like. He wondered if his father was feeling that way. As the officer gave him a one-hundred-dollar speeding ticket, Mr. Maxwell had been terribly polite. "Yes, Officer." And "No,

Officer." And "I'm sorry, Officer. It won't happen again." Simon hadn't known which was worse, the sight of his father getting caught breaking the law or the awful, polite way he'd talked to the policeman.

Simon looked at Mattie nervously. Why didn't she pull off the road? But his great-aunt continued driving merrily down the road, seemingly unconcerned about the lights flashing inches behind her car. Simon peeked out the back. He could see the policeman's face growing stern and red. Suddenly, the patrol car pulled out beside Aunt Mattie. The policeman gestured with his arm to her to pull over. Mattie gave him an icy look.

At last, the police car swerved in front of them, forcing Aunt Mattie off the road, onto the dirt shoulder. She stopped the car, and the police cruiser pulled up a few feet in front of them.

Now she's really gonna get it, thought Simon. Reckless driving, refusing to stop for a police officer, speeding, resisting arrest. He was sure they put you in prison for that. Maybe they'd arrest her on the spot. He glanced at his aunt with deep concern. But she looked neither worried nor angry. She looked stern.

Suddenly, Mattie turned off the engine. Before the policeman could budge from his car, Mattie hopped out and strode briskly over to his door. She rapped smartly on his window with her car keys. The policeman, who was talking on his car radio, looked at her in astonishment. He hung up his radio receiver and rolled down the window.

"Young man," said Mattie, "what on earth do you mean by driving like that?"

"What?" said the officer, a look of disbelief on his face.

"You heard me," snapped Mattie. "You were tailgating

me—a very dangerous practice to drive so close to another car. And then you passed me in a 'no passing' zone. Are you aware that you passed me on a solid yellow line?"

"What?" said the officer again.

"And all that gesturing and swerving in front of me like that! Why, we could have had a terrible accident!" Mattie paused and peered inside the patrol car. "Young man, are you aware that your seat belt is not fastened? Well"—she straightened up—"I'm afraid I'm going to have to take your name and badge number and report you to the police."

"What?" said the policeman again. He was beginning to sound like a broken record. "But, lady, I *am* the police." He looked around, as if hoping another patrol car might be coming to his rescue.

"You heard me," said Mattie briskly, taking a pad and pencil from her purse. She licked the end of the pencil. "Name and badge number, please."

"Now listen here, lady—" said the officer.

"And after that I'll need to see your driver's license and car registration. I urge you to cooperate. Otherwise, I might have to make a citizen's arrest."

From his seat in the car, Simon watched in amazement as the police officer climbed out of his cruiser. He handed his badge, license, and registration over to Mattie. Next he closed his eyes and touched his finger to his nose. Then Mattie had him walk a straight line along the edge of the road.

"What's she doing?" Simon asked Philbert.

"Sobriety test," answered Philbert, as if he'd seen this sort of thing before.

"What's that?"

"It's a test the police give you—touch your nose, walk a straight line—to make sure you haven't been drinkin' alcohol. Not supposed to drink and drive, you see."

"But why's *she* doing it to *him*?"

"Well, you gotta admit he was drivin' pretty strangely. Tailgatin' and flashin' his lights, and cuttin' in front of us."

"But that's what the police *always* do when you're supposed to pull over."

"Really?" said Philbert, sounding interested. "Darn stupid way to carry on, if you ask me."

Just then, Mattie returned to the car. She squeezed herself into the seat, started the engine, and pulled the car back onto the road. They passed the police officer. He was sitting in his cruiser, resting his head limply on the steering wheel.

"Just fancy," said Mattie, as they lurched along. "*He* was going to give *me* a ticket!"

"What happened?" asked Simon, still unable to believe Mattie hadn't been hauled away in handcuffs.

"Oh, he was such a sweet young man," said Mattie. "I let him off with a warning."

Have a Good One

At length, they arrived at the store. It was in a mall that stretched off into the distance. Aunt Mattie drove around, looking for a parking space amid the sea of cars that glittered in the sun. Finally, they found a woman who was leaving, and Aunt Mattie waited patiently for her to pull out.

"Hate the mall," grumped Uncle Philbert in the front seat. "Why couldn't we go to the five-and-dime on Main Street?"

"I would have, dear, but they closed when the mall opened." Aunt Mattie turned to Simon in the back. "Why, three years ago, this used to be apple orchards and ponds. The town had one store, the five-and-dime. It had everything you needed, and you could be done in about four minutes."

"Now we have a hundred and fifty stores to shop at," groaned Philbert. "I can never find what I need, and it takes two hours."

Just as the woman pulled out of Mattie's parking space, a little red MG coming from the other direction cut in front of Mattie and zoomed into the spot they had been waiting for. A man jumped out of the sports car, refused to look at them, and strode off to the stores.

Simon's father would have been furious if that had happened to him. Mattie just smiled.

"Everyone's in such a terrible hurry these days," she said. "Never a wonderful hurry or a delicious hurry. Always a terrible hurry. It's the reason most people forget their manners. Not to worry. There's room for both of us." And she pulled the heavy car up behind the snappy little MG until their bumpers were touching. Mattie's car stuck far out into the lane, but she didn't seem to mind. "Off we go," she said cheerfully.

"But Aunt Mattie," said Simon, looking back at the red sports car, wedged between Mattie's car and the car in front of it. "That man's stuck in that space until we come back."

"Is he?" asked his aunt innocently. "Why, yes, I do believe he is. As I said, people are in much too much of a hurry these days. It's bad for the heart."

As they walked past the red car, Uncle Philbert gave it a little pat on the hood. Just a friendly little pat, or so it seemed to Simon at the time.

They entered the cavelike mall, going from bright sunshine to the artificial glow of indoor lighting. Mattie seemed to know where she was going. She directed Philbert to a hardware store, then quickly found a clothing store for Simon. In a matter of a few minutes, they picked out two T-shirts, a pair of jeans, and some sneakers that suited Simon just fine.

Then they went to wait for Philbert by a little pond in the center of the mall. Simon sat beneath some fake trees that seemed to grow well in the fake sunlight, and watched the fake ducks floating in the water. At last, Philbert showed up, looking extremely cross. "It was bad enough getting lost," he fumed. "But what I really can't stand is all those people telling me to have a nice day. Maybe I want to have a *bad* day! And the sales clerk hands me the lawn mower handle in a little bag and says, 'Have a good one.'

" 'Have a good *what?*' I say.

" 'Huh?' says the clerk.

" 'Have a good nap?' I say. 'A good trip? A good *what* exactly do you want me to have?'

" 'Oh, you know,' says the clerk. 'I meant, like, enjoy.'

"Now, I ask you," sputtered Uncle Philbert, "does she really think I'm gonna *enjoy* a lawn mower handle?"

Mattie laughed and led Simon and the still-sputtering Uncle Philbert back to the car, where a small drama awaited them. The owner of the MG was pacing beside his car.

"I've been waiting for twenty minutes," he shouted when he saw them. "What do you mean by parking behind me? People like you shouldn't be allowed on the road. Now move your car—I'm in a hurry."

He jumped into his car, and Mattie peered in his window.

"Very boring," she said pleasantly, "always to be in a terrible hurry. Myself, I always try to be a little late. Makes it more fun. You should try it someday."

The man ignored this advice and attempted to start his car instead. But the only noise that came from his engine was a series of strange clicks. He groaned and tried again. Nothing happened. The man jumped out and opened the hood. Simon saw Mattie and Philbert exchange a look.

Simon's aunt walked back to her car, but rather than getting inside, she took a screwdriver out of the trunk and returned to the sports car.

"Keep out of my way, you old cow," said the man as he peered under the hood.

"I think you'll find it's the solenoid," said Mattie mildly. "A loose wire, no doubt."

"Oh, right," said the man with a sneer. Ignoring Mattie, he climbed behind the wheel and tried to start the car again. Mattie took the screwdriver, leaned under the hood, and fiddled with something. The engine sprang to life.

"What the—" exclaimed the driver.

"The solenoid," said Mattie. "It's a common problem with the 1967 MG."

And she got back into her car and drove home.

Super Hero

In his afternoons, Simon hung out at the barn.

He watched the llamas, the llamas watched him, and they had spitting contests. During un-lessons, Uncle Philbert had tried to teach Simon the Fine Art of Spitting, but Simon had never quite gotten the knack of it. The llamas won the spitting contests easily. They could spit farther and seldom missed their target. Simon's attempts to retaliate generally ended up with spittle dribbling off his chin. He could practically see the llamas laughing at him. Shirt after shirt was subjected to Matilda's bottle of Surefire Llama Spit Stain Remover. But Simon didn't give up.

One day he was sitting on the fence rail, watching the llamas eat. Simon had learned that the way to challenge llamas to a spitting contest was to stare hard at them. It seemed, for some reason, to annoy them. Now Mr. Crude was watching Simon out of the corner of his eye. He was waiting, Simon could tell, for the right moment to strike. As he sat, Simon rehearsed Uncle Philbert's advice.

"Use that gap in your front teeth," Philbert had told him. "Your orthodontist may hate it, but it's great for spittin'."

Simon was ready when Mr. Crude raised his head and drew a bead on him. Fixing the llama with a steady stare, Simon placed his tongue behind his front teeth, aimed in the direction of Mr. Crude, and spat as hard as he could.

This time, instead of the shotgun spray he usually produced, a big gob of spit shot from between Simon's teeth like a bullet. It hit Mr. Crude right on the nose. The llama couldn't have looked more surprised if Simon had flattened him with a fire hose. Simon laughed so hard that he fell off the fence.

From that day on, Simon was unbeatable. Soon the llamas edged nervously away when they saw him coming. Even Mr. Ugly knew that if he tried any funny stuff with Simon, he'd get it right between the eyes.

But as much as he liked the llamas, Simon spent most of his free time with Hero. Twice a day, he brought the chestnut horse his grain and hay. Mattie was happy to have him feed Hero, and after Simon had begged her enough times, she agreed to let Simon brush the horse, too.

"I never bothered with grooming him," she told Simon, leading him to a dusty tack box at the back of the stable. "I figured he didn't need people fussing over him and making his life a misery. What he needs is freedom. Besides, I was too worried about getting kicked. That horse doesn't trust people much, and who can blame him? Now, you keep clear of his back legs, and don't let him nip you."

Inside the box, Simon found curry combs and body brushes, hoof picks, oil, saddle soaps—everything for grooming a horse. Best of all, at the bottom of the box, was a tattered book, *You and Your Horse*. Here, Simon found advice and illustrations on everything to do with horse care and riding.

Simon knew better than to rush things with Hero. So for the first few days, he simply fed the horse, watching him over the top of the stall door and talking to him while the horse snuffed and blew and rolled his eyes up to watch the boy without lifting his head from the grain bin.

Every morning, Mattie would fill Simon's pockets with carrots. By the third day, when Simon arrived, Hero was waiting, his head resting on the door, looking for his treat. Simon played dumb: "What are you lookin' at me like that for, you silly beast?" The horse ducked his head and butted Simon in the chest, then started a snuffling search of his pockets.

"Okay, okay!" Simon laughed, producing the carrots and remembering to hold his hand flat to avoid the horse's teeth, the way it said to in the book. When Hero was done with the carrots, he thrust his head into Simon's neck and started chomping on the collar buttons of his shirt. His whiskers and soft skin tickled, but Simon held very still, so as not to startle him. Hero kept his

head there, against Simon's chest, while Simon found the spots by his ears that needed scratching, and Hero blew his hot breath into Simon's sweater and nibbled on buttons and tilted his ears forward to catch the flow of words that tumbled from Simon. And they stood like that for half an hour while Simon told Hero everything. He told him how much he admired him for bucking off his old owner. He told him that if he had anything to say about it, no one would ever hurt Hero again. He told him about himself, and about his mother and father. He told him about school and the other kids in his class, about Mrs. Biggs, his teacher, and about how he hoped spring vacation would never end. And about how he wanted Hero to let him brush him.

After four days, Simon decided the moment had finally come. He got out the grooming tools and slowly opened the stall door. Hero backed nervously away. Simon wondered if he should tie Hero's head with the halter hanging by the door. Instead, he kept up a steady stream of talk, trying to calm the horse as he looked him over.

Grooming Hero would be no small job. The horse hadn't been properly brushed in a year. His dull brown coat, thick and shaggy from the winter, was full of burrs and caked with mud. His tail and mane were snarled and filthy.

Simon leaned against Hero and, taking the rubber curry comb, started work on the matted, dirty coat. He worked slowly from head to tail, rubbing in circles, raising clouds of dust and horse hair as he went.

At first, Simon worried that Hero would get fed up, the way Simon used to when his mother had given *him* a haircut. But he soon discovered Hero's secret: the big lunk actually loved being brushed. The shivering and prancing, which had started when Simon first entered the stall, stopped the moment he laid a brush to Hero's neck. From time to time, the horse lifted his head off the stall door, turned to watch Simon at work, and nickered.

"What's the matter, you big dope?" asked Simon happily at these times. "Did I miss a spot or something?"

The job took Simon several hours. When he had finished currying, he tackled the mane and tail. The tail was so tangled, he could only comb it out a few inches at a time. Then, dipping the body brush in water, he worked on the snarled mane until it lay in neat black strands on Hero's neck. Next he took a soft cloth, wet it, and rubbed and polished Hero's whole body. He took a can of hoof oil from the tack box and brushed each of Hero's hooves with the shiny liquid. Last of all—studying the drawings in the book—he made a stab at braiding the tail. It didn't look nearly as fine as the tail of the horse in the illustration, but Simon had to admit it was pretty fantastic.

When it was all over, Simon was filthy, and exhausted. But the horse was transformed. The shaggy wild beast was gone. In his place was a sleek and shining animal. His chestnut coat shone like burnished metal. His polished hooves gleamed like black coal. And his dark mane shimmered in the light. Hero gave a great snort—almost a sigh—of happiness and laid his head over Simon's shoulder. And Simon stood there, loving the sheer weight of the animal and not wanting to move.

Finally, he pulled himself away.

"I'll be right back," he promised the horse.

Inside the farmhouse, he found Aunt Mattie sitting on

the couch, with several cats sleeping on her lap and shoulder.

"It's a beautiful day today, Simon," she said. "Would you like to play golf?"

"No," said Simon hastily. "I—"

"Good," said Mattie. "Neither would I."

It was only afterward that he realized that the old Simon would never have answered his aunt that way. But he didn't stop to think about it then.

"I've got something to show you. Come sit on the porch."

Mattie shooed Sugar off the porch, plucked a peacock out of her rocking chair, and did as she was told. Simon sprinted back into the barn. He grabbed the halter off the hook, slid it over Hero's head, and led him out of the barn, prancing excitedly—the horse, that is, not Simon.

When he came in sight of the porch, his aunt gasped and sat straight up in her chair.

"My dear, where did you get that absolutely divine horse?"

"That's Hero, Aunt Mattie."

"Never!" shouted Mattie. "Hero is a scruffy, filthy old rag. This—why, this creature is a gorgeous thoroughbred from some racetrack."

Simon laughed and rubbed Hero's neck. For his part, Hero bent down and ate one of Aunt Mattie's bright orange tulips.

Interrup–

The following day, Simon was helping Aunt Mattie feed the llamas. Just as Mattie was emptying some grain into their trough, one of the smaller ones leaned down and nipped her broad bottom. Mattie shrieked loudly and shook a finger at them.

"Miserable ingrates! Mangy, mucculent misfits! Have you no gratitude? Biting the hand that feeds you!"

"Bottom," said Simon seriously.

"What?"

"They didn't bite the *hand* that feeds them; they bit the *bottom*."

Mattie nearly burst, laughing at Simon's little joke. She liked it so much that she repeated it that night at dinner to Uncle Philbert. Philbert looked surprised. "I'm sure you ain't allowed to say the word *bottom* in your own house."

Simon looked down at his plate of peach pie. "I'm not," he said. Nor was he allowed to say *butt* or *bum*. He had to say *backside*, or, worse, *derrière*. "My parents say it's not a nice word."

To his surprise, Philbert fixed Simon with a stern look. "Simon," he said, "I been meanin' to talk to you about your language. There's some words we just won't tolerate in this house, and that's one of them."

Simon blushed a bright crimson. "I'm sorry. I won't ever say *bottom* again—" he started to say. But Philbert interrupted him.

"*Bottom*—heck. I ain't talkin' about *bottom*. You can say *bottom* till you're blue in the gills if you like."

"Then what word *do* you mean?"

"*Nice*," said Uncle Philbert, rolling his eyes and pulling at his hair. "I hate that word. How was your day?" he continued in a high voice. "Nice. How was the movie? Nice. I had a nice time. Did you have a nice time? We all had a nice time. Have a nice day. What does *nice* mean? Does it mean exciting? Or relaxing? Or profitable? Nice—hah!"

"I wonder . . . ," murmured Mattie. "Let's see what it actually means." She reached behind her chair to a dishwasher Simon had never noticed before and pulled out the bottom rack. It was full of books and pads and notebooks stacked like plates. The silverware holder was full of pens and pencils, scissors, rulers, and bottles of glue. Mattie noticed Simon's stare. "This is my desk," she explained simply. And then she added, "Make sure you never turn the dishwasher on by mistake someday."

She pulled a tattered red *Webster's Dictionary* from the front rack, found the page she wanted, and read: " 'Nice: (adjective) dissolute'—oh, that means *very* badly behaved! That's the first meaning. The next meaning is 'fussy, persnickety.' And the third meaning is 'skillful.' There you go. Think of *that* the next time you use the word *nice!*"

"Have a very badly behaved day," said Simon solemnly.

"Have a fussy day," said Uncle Philbert.

"Have a skillful day," added Aunt Mattie.

"And speaking of bad language," said Philbert to Simon as soon as they had all stopped giggling, "somebody really needs to teach you how to cuss."

Mattie looked surprised. "I thought *you* were teaching him how to cuss."

"I thought you were."

Simon grinned excitedly. "Are you going to teach me how to swear? Really?"

Philbert gave him a disgusted look. "Not *swear*, Mr. Mush for Brains. *Cuss.* Any moron can swear. But it takes real genius to cuss. Your aunt is a champion cusser."

"Thank you, Bert," said Mattie, looking modestly down at her plate. She smoothed her place mat. "You're not half-bad yourself."

"I don't understand," said Simon. "What's the difference between cussing and swearing?"

"Swearin'," said Philbert, as if explaining to a two-year-old, "is just usin' bad language—you know, the kind of garbage you hear every day from some loudmouth on the street who doesn't have any imagination. Cussin' . . . well, cussin' is an art. You ever hear your aunt Mattie talk to the llamas?"

"Yes."

"That's cussin'."

"Or," added Mattie, "the way your great-uncle here talks to the farm machines. That's cussing."

"I see," said Simon, trying to remember what Mattie had called the llamas. Mangy something misfits. Mucculent. "Mangy, mucculent misfits." What did that mean? He reached for the dictionary.

"Pass the cinnamon," said Philbert, taking a large bite of pie. Simon, his head in his book, passed the cinnamon shaker absentmindedly to Uncle Philbert.

Aunt Mattie did not keep salt and pepper shakers on the table like most people. Well, she did have salt and pepper shakers. But they didn't have salt and pepper in them. They had cinnamon and Parmesan cheese. Or brown sugar and chili powder. "Why on earth would anyone want to put crystals of salt or crushed pepper seeds on *all* their food *all* the time?" Mattie said in surprise once when Simon asked her about this. And, as usual, Simon could think of no reason why he should put pepper or salt on all his food and not cinnamon or cheese.

Had Simon been at home, his mother would have reminded him that it was not polite to read at the table, and he would have had to put the dictionary away. But at Aunt Mattie's, it was quite acceptable to read at mealtime. Frequently, whole meals would pass with the three of them deep in their own books. (Philbert was working his way through the *Encyclopaedia Britannica*; currently he was on *J*. Mattie was reading something called *Zen and the Art of Motorcycle Maintenance*. And Simon was reading everything he could put his hands on that had to do with horses.) Often one of them would read a favorite part out loud. They'd all laugh and then go back to their books.

"And while we're on the subject of language," said

Philbert, pushing away his pie plate and reaching for a bowl of Cheerios, "there's altogether too much Not Speakin' Before Bein' Spoken To goin' on."

"Excuse me?" asked Simon, looking up from the dictionary. He had just discovered that *mucculent* meant "slimy," and was thinking of lots of good ways to use it. "Isn't it bad manners to—"

"And," Aunt Mattie added, "there's entirely not enough Interrupting."

Uncle Philbert paused, his spoon of Cheerios halfway to his mouth.

"There she goes again," he said to Simon.

"What?"

"Interruptin'," said Uncle Philbert. "She is *always* interrup—"

"Am I?" said Mattie. "I never noticed."

"My mother says it's rude to interrupt," said Simon shyly.

"Well, once again, Simon, I can tell you that interrupting is all a matter of what you're used to," said his great-aunt, giving each of them a ferocious stare. "In some places, like England, people always interrupt one another. You see, if the conversation is interesting enough, people can't wait to start talking. It adds excitement.

"But in this country, for some strange reason, it's always considered rude. You have to wait till some old windbag is done repeating himself five or six times." She glared at Philbert. "And then, when you're sure it's safe, you may speak. In my humble opinion, it is far ruder to be the old windbag than to be the interrupter. Because by the time it's safe for anyone else to open his mouth, he's forgotten what he wanted to say. Or wandered off to talk to the cats."

"So interrupting is *not* rude?" asked Simon, unable to believe his ears.

"Well, sometimes it is," said Philbert, "and—"

"Sometimes it isn't," Mattie interrupted. She smiled at Simon. "Why don't you give it a try?"

"Me? Try interrupting?" Simon was shocked.

"Yes," said his aunt. "You need practice to unlearn old habits and learn some new ones."

"Give the boy a chance," said Uncle Philbert. "He's got to get used to the idea. Interruptin' is not a skill you can just pick up overnight."

It was true. It was one thing to be told it was okay to interrupt, for example. It was quite another to do it in real life. Over the next few days, Simon made an effort. Time after time, he failed. Then one evening at dinner, Uncle Philbert was telling a story about how he got kicked by a mule.

"Next thing you know," said Philbert, "that ornery critter curled his ugly lips back and—"

Simon saw an opening.

"Pass the cinnamon, please," he interrupted.

"Wrong!" said Philbert. "Rude!"

Simon looked bewildered.

"It shows you weren't listening to him," explained Mattie. "Now try again."

Philbert resumed the story.

"And the mule opened his mouth, and—"

"Once I saw a horse bite someone," said Simon, swinging (as it were) wildly.

"Wrong!" said Mattie and Philbert together. "That sounds like you can't wait to talk about *yourself*. If, for example, you interrupted to ask what color the mule's teeth were," Mattie explained patiently, "now *that* would be fine. It shows you are so interested in what he is saying, you can't wait to know more."

"Okay," said Simon. "I think I get it now. Try me again." He bent over his plate, concentrating hard. This time, he would do it right! He felt inspiration filling him. He breathed deeply and slowly.

"And after he planted his feet on my backside,"

Uncle Philbert concluded his story, "I pulled up my shirt, and danged if he hadn't kicked me so hard, there was the shape of his ornery hoof right there on my skin. Like a tattoo. Why, you could even count the nails in his h—"

"I hope you sold that no-good, hairy troglodyte to the glue factory!" Simon cried.

There was a moment's hush. Mattie and Philbert exchanged glances.

"Yes!" they said. Philbert looked awed. "Boy," he said solemnly, "first off, you interrupted beautifully—perfect timing, really perfect. And then you threw in a batch of really fine cuss words for good measure. Hang me if you ain't a prodigy. Prod-i-gy." Mattie gave him a second helping of pie. Philbert sat back, put his handkerchief to his lips, and burped. Simon jabbed his thumb into his forehead. He went happily around the table, giving everyone a playful punch in the arm.

He couldn't have done it at home. But he wasn't at home now, was he?

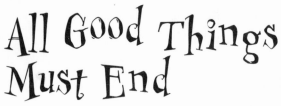

Several nights later, Simon lay sprawled on the couch, enjoying the horsey smell that wafted off his clothes. Some people—his father for one—might have said he was being idle. (George Maxwell was never idle. He was always fixing storm windows or looking things up in dictionaries or making lists.)

Simon might have looked idle. But actually, he was thinking. He was thinking about burping. Despite all of Uncle Philbert's un-lessons, the one area in which Simon had made no progress at all was with the Gentle Art of Burping. "You ain't a proper kid," said Philbert, "unless'n you can burp."

Uncle Philbert was able to produce a burp at a moment's notice—long burps, short burps, delicate burps, disgusting burps. He coached Simon hour after hour: "It's all in the throat, my boy. You tighten up those throat muscles, you see, like this, and then suck in real hard.

Then let 'er rip. Be sure you cover your mouth, son. Ain't nobody wants to look at your tonsils when you're burpin'."

But Simon couldn't ever seem to manage more than a fake-sounding croak.

That night, he lay there on the couch, enjoying the horsey smell, and thought, If I could just learn to burp, then everything would be perfect.

At that very moment, the phone rang. Both Mattie and Philbert looked startled. Simon realized it was the first time the telephone had rung since he'd been there.

"Botheration," said Mattie, putting down her book. "You answer it, Bert. I've got a parrot on my shoulder." As indeed she did.

Philbert leaped up from his end of the couch and began rummaging under the piles of magazines. The phone continued ringing, making an oddly muffled sound.

"Now just where *is* that phone?" asked Philbert.

"Don't know, dear," said Mattie, looking around vaguely. "The last time I saw it, it was under that crate of cat food."

"Well, it's not there now," huffed Uncle Philbert. "Oh, the devil take it!" he said, sinking back onto the couch. At that moment, the phone rang one last time, and Philbert jumped up again. The telephone, in fact, was under the very sofa cushion he was sitting on. It was an old-fashioned phone, the kind with a heavy, curved receiver and a round metal dial. Philbert snatched up the receiver, holding it out between thumb and forefinger as if it were some particularly poisonous sort of viper.

"I already got one!" he shouted into it, and stuffed the machine back under the cushion. "It's probably just

someone trying to sell me a trip to Florida," Philbert explained. "I already been once. 1937. Didn't like it then, wouldn't like it now."

The phone rang again. This time, Mattie answered it, while Runcible teetered on her shoulder.

"Hell-ow!" she said. She had probably meant to say hello in the normal way, but as she opened her mouth, Runcible had dug her claws straight into Aunt Mattie's shoulder. And then, as the other person started to speak, Runcible leaned over and shouted into the phone, "Shut your trap!"

"Just a minute," said Mattie, trying to muzzle the parrot with one hand. "Simon, dear, it's for you."

It was Simon's mother. For a moment, neither one of them could think of anything to say. Simon was shocked to realize that he hadn't missed his mother or father once, after that first morning. Hadn't even thought about them. Now for an instant, he had trouble imagining what they looked like, where they were standing while they spoke on the phone, what day it was.

Simon's mother was speechless for different reasons. At last she said, "Simon? What was all that about? Hello? Simon?"

"Hello, Mother. . . . Oh, that? That was just Runcible. The parrot. . . . No, *that* was Uncle Philbert. He must have, um, thought it was a wrong number." As he spoke, Simon sat up straighter and straighter. "Of course I'm all right. Why wouldn't I be? Yes, Mother. . . . Yes, Mother. . . . Tomorrow. The ten o'clock train. See you then. . . . Yes. . . . Good-bye, Mother."

He hung up the phone and sat stunned for a few minutes.

"Going home?" asked Philbert.

Simon nodded dumbly. He couldn't even think about it.

"That must have been your mother, then," said Mattie briskly. "And how is she?"

"I don't know. We couldn't talk for long"—here Simon could not keep a slightly sarcastic note from creeping into his voice—"because it seems Aunt Bea and Uncle Fred are still there, and they were expecting an important call and we mustn't tie up the phone."

Mattie gave him a long glance. "You have to take the train tomorrow?"

"Yes."

"Well, time just flew, didn't it?"

Simon was silent.

"But you must be eager to get home?" asked his great-aunt gently.

At last he said, "Do I have to say the polite thing? Or the truth? Because the truth is, I don't want to go home. It's different here. I like it. Home is . . . Well, Aunt Bea and Uncle Fred are still there. Parker is still in my room. I'm going to have to sleep on the couch, I bet, while smelly old Parker messes up my room."

Simon kicked at a stack of old phone books as he talked—they were being used as a coffee table. Runcible fluttered up to the rubber tree on the ceiling.

"And I don't want to go back to school again. I hate Mrs. Biggs. And all the kids at school hate me. And . . ." As tears of self-pity filled his eyes, Simon got to his feet. "I'm going up to bed," he said. "Good-night." And he took the stairs two at a time.

It was only after he'd finished brushing his teeth that Simon realized what else had been bugging him about the conversation with his mother. She hadn't even bothered to ask after Uncle Philbert and Aunt Mattie. Not a word. As he lay in bed pondering this, there was a knock on the door, and Mattie came in.

"I know boys don't like to be kissed," she said, "but for once you have to be polite to your old auntie and let me give you a last good-night kiss."

She bent over quickly and kissed him on the forehead, and before she could straighten up, Simon grabbed her hand.

"There are two things I forgot to say," he said. "First, I forgot to say that the real reason I don't want to go home is because I had such a good time here—"

"I know that, Simon," said Mattie with a smile.

Simon took a deep breath. "And the other thing is that my mother sends her love."

70

Mattie stood looking at him for a spell, the smile still lingering on her lips. Then she bent over and brushed the hair out of his eyes. "Thank you for that little lie, my dear."

And before Simon could say anything, she had gone.

The next morning was miserable. As a special treat for breakfast, Uncle Philbert had made Simon his Twenty-Four-Alarm Chili and Beans ("guaranteed to fry your innards"). Stayed up all night letting it simmer, he did. But Simon had no appetite.

When Philbert saw he wasn't eating, he slapped him on the back.

"That's right, boy!" he said. "Never pretend you like someone's cookin' when you don't. Try eatin' something you hate and you'll lose your lunch all over the table. Nothing, *nothing*, is worse manners than barfing at the table."

Simon remembered what Philbert had taught him during the long lesson on Table Manners: never eat something you can't stand, but always thank the cook for going to the trouble.

"I love your chili, Uncle Philbert. You know I do. It's just . . . I don't feel hungry right now."

"Of course you don't," said Aunt Mattie. "Why don't you run along and get packed?"

So Simon got up from the table. He didn't say, "May I be excused?" because the first time he'd asked that, Philbert had nearly split himself from laughing. "Excused for what? Finishing your meal? Being alive?"

Instead of packing, however, he ran out to the paddock and climbed up on the fence. He put his fingers in his mouth and gave a shrill whistle. Hero looked up from the other side of the field and cantered over. He nearly knocked Simon over backward searching his pockets for carrots. While he chewed, Simon talked. Simon told him he was leaving. He might never see Hero again. He rubbed Hero's ears and told him there was one more thing he wanted to do before he left.

Simon jumped down, walked to Hero's side, and pushed the horse gently until his broad flank was against the fence. Then Simon mounted the fence. "I want you to let me ride you just once. Just for a moment. That's all," said Simon, talking gently into Hero's ear. The horse shuddered, lowered his head, and pawed at the ground. But he stayed put. Slowly, Simon lifted one leg and slid it partway across Hero's back. He let it rest there a moment while Hero got used to the feel of it. The horse was holding stock-still now, as if he sensed that Simon had never been on a horse before. Simon slid his whole weight onto Hero's back, clinging with one hand to the fence and keeping the other around Hero's neck. Then he let go of the fence, and he was sitting on Hero's back. Simon felt all the horse's muscles bunching under him, as if it was taking every ounce of Hero's strength just to hold still.

Trying hard to remember what the book had said

about riding, Simon nudged Hero with his heel, all the while talking quietly into his ear. Hero took a step forward alongside the fence, then another. When they were halfway around the paddock, Simon leaned forward and thrust his heels into Hero's side. The horse went straight from a walk into a long, slow canter. To Simon's own

amazement, he didn't slide off into the mud. Somehow he stayed up there, clinging to Hero's mane, until they had made a complete circle of the paddock. Hero slowed to a halt before the fence, and Simon slid off his back.

"It's our secret," said Simon. "No one will ever know." And then he gave him one last pat, and one last carrot, and went inside to pack.

Saying good-bye to Raspberry was almost as hard as saying good-bye to Hero. The cat jumped onto his bed while he folded his clothes, and rolled around on them, as if trying to stop Simon from packing. Each time Simon bent over his suitcase, Raspberry walked under him, his tail brushing Simon's face, his head turned to look into Simon's eyes, a loud purr rumbling in his chest. For an instant, Simon toyed with the idea of packing Raspberry in his suitcase, too. He hugged him to his head one last time, then darted downstairs.

Here, he said good-bye to Runcible ("Good-bye, good riddance," the parrot answered); and the peacocks, who were preening by the porch; and Sugar, who took one last lump; and Mr. Ugly, who exchanged one last spitball with him; and finally, Uncle Philbert, who said it would be real nice to have his sofa back, thanks very much, and to be sure to remember to write a thank-you note, hardy-har-har.

They were, of course, late getting to the station, but not late enough, for the train was also late. Simon and Mattie stood silently, neither one feeling much like making up polite conversation, until Simon heard the train approaching.

Then he turned to his great-aunt and, speaking quickly, said, "Aunt Mattie, why is it that my family doesn't like you? I used to think it was because you were a witch."

"Really?" said Mattie, a gleam of humor in her eyes. "Tell me, what do they say about me?"

"They don't say anything—that's just the problem. They say you're 'you know.' What do they mean by that?"

She laughed and handed him a package. "Here's some lunch for you. A piece of lemon meringue pie. And for dessert, a pickle sandwich."

The train had pulled into the station. Mattie folded Simon in that hug she had, the one that smelled of licorice and lavender, and picked up his suitcase. She bustled him onto the train. But he turned to look at her from the steps as the train pulled out.

"What do they mean?" he demanded.

"Didn't anyone teach you not to ask so many questions?" Mattie laughed. She waved and blew him a kiss.

Be Nice

His mother was waiting for him as the train pulled in, an anxious expression on her face. She looked as if she'd been there a long time. Poor Mother, thought Simon, realizing as he did so that he'd never felt that particular emotion before. She gave him a long hug, rumpled his hair, smoothed it down again.

"How brown you are! You look so . . . different. Did you have a nice time? Gracious, whatever happened to your shirt?"

"Oh, that's just llama spit. You see, the Stain Remover only kind of spread it a—"

"Llama spit! And the buttons are all missing!"

"Oh, Hero, the horse, ate them. You see—"

Mrs. Maxwell covered her ears. "I don't think I want to know *any* more. You poor boy. Thank goodness you're home safe and sound."

Simon sighed. "I'm sorry I'm late—" he began. And then he stopped. "No, I'm not. You should do what Aunt

Mattie does. Try being a little late all the time. It makes things more interesting."

"What?" asked his mother.

"Like, well, what did you do while you were waiting for me?"

"Do? I checked the timetable. I paced. I looked at my watch."

Simon realized that this wasn't going to be as easy as he'd thought.

"I don't know what Aunt Matilda has been telling you, Simon, but being late shows a lack of respect. It's just plain rude."

"But—"

"I hope I won't have any of that around Aunt Bea and Uncle Fred."

"No, Mother."

He threw his duffel into the back of the old station wagon.

"Where's Father?" he asked. He thought his father might have come to the station to meet him.

"He wanted to be here, but his boss—you know, Mr. Hackney—called and asked him to attend a special meeting. He won't get home till after you're in bed, I'm afraid."

"On a *Sunday*?"

"Yes, I know, it's unfair, but he's working very hard to get this promotion. He's made up a very clever ad campaign for the chewing-gum magnate."

"What is it?"

"Well, he wants to call the gum Dubble Bubble. And the ad shows some witches stirring a pot, and all sorts of bubbles are coming out, and they're singing this jingle: 'Double, double toil and trouble; Fire burn and . . .

Dubble Bubble.' It comes from a Shakespeare play. The client is going to love it."

Simon laughed. "It's good."

"Yes, even Uncle Fred and Aunt Bea thought it was funny."

Simon's smile turned to a frown. "Why are Uncle Fred and Aunt Bea still here?" he asked. "You promised they would only stay two weeks."

"Now, dear, I know it's exasperating, but imagine how they must feel—their kitchen still isn't done; the workmen are way behind schedule. They can't move back in with the place full of plaster dust and no stove or water, can they?"

"Does this mean I get to sleep on the couch? And horrible, fat old Parker is still in my room?"

"Simon!" Her voice was shocked. "I won't have you talking that way about your own cousin." Then she softened. "I know it's hard for you. But what else can we do? We can't ask them to leave. And it will only be for another week or so. And you mustn't call him 'fat old Parker.' He's slightly overweight, but that's not his fault. It's genetic."

"A *week*, Mother? I can't bear it for that long! It's not fair. Why don't they go stay in a hotel, like we did when our house was being done over?"

"Well, I . . ." But his mother seemed to have no answer to this question. "We just can't ask them to leave," she said. "And that's all there is to it. Here we are. There's Aunt Bea. Now remember to shake their hands. And be nice and polite."

Simon did shake hands with Aunt Bea, thankful that he didn't have to kiss her.

"Hello, Aunt Bea. Yes, the train trip was fine. Yes, it was a little late."

Aunt Bea was a tall, big-toothed woman with extremely red hair. Her voice, while not exactly loud, had a piercing quality to it that meant it traveled. Simon guessed there would be no room in their small house that would be out of range of her voice. He remembered his mother saying that Aunt Bea really didn't like children, and that was another reason for Simon to be away while she was here.

"You've grown very tall," said Aunt Bea with a "let's get this over with" kind of tone in her voice. "I'm sure you had a nice time in the country."

"Very nice," mumbled Simon. "Very dissolute."

"Good. Don't mumble," said his aunt, already turning away to talk to his mother. "Now, Shirley, when is the cleaning woman coming? Parker's asthma is really acting up, and I'm sure it's because of all the dust."

His mother laughed nervously. "I'm such a terrible housekeeper," she said.

At that moment, Uncle Fred appeared. A large man with very red cheeks, he shook Simon's hand, and then, with the air of having made a major discovery, told him that he had grown.

Simon admitted that this was probably true, and then, when it was clear that Uncle Fred had run out of conversation, Simon took the opportunity to escape to his room. He flung open the door with relief.

"Hey!" said a voice from the bed. "Don't you know it's rude to barge into somebody's room without knocking?"

It was Parker. The chubby older boy was curled up in a

sleeping bag on Simon's bed. He was in his pajamas and
was reading Simon's comics. Simon's jaw dropped in disbelief—not because Parker had pilfered his beloved
comic book collection, but because of the room. It was

totally bare. Gone were the curtains and rug, the books and bookshelves, the model airplanes, the rock collection, the goldfish bowl, the Pirates banners, the Wayne Gretzky posters, the stuffed armchair. Nothing was left but a stripped bed, a barren desk, and a tiny TV set.

"Where's all my stuff?" yelled Simon.

"In storage," said Parker, not bothering to look up from his comic—or rather, Simon's comic. He pulled a handful of Cheesios from a bag beside him and stuffed them in his mouth. "Took your mom a whole day to do it," he said, spraying little Cheesio crumbs over the sheets as he spoke.

"Why? Why is it in storage?"

"Because of my asthma, you know," said Parker. "Too much dust in here. We had to scrub the whole room, and all your stuff was in the way. Dust magnets, most of it. Made me cough." He gave Simon a wicked smile, and produced a little fake wheeze to show what he meant. "Oh, don't worry, you'll get it back when I leave. And I saved out your X-Men collection." He lifted a pillow to show Simon a stack of comics, his precious comics, all rumpled and torn, their covers coming off.

What Simon wanted to do was to murder Parker. He wondered briefly if it was against the law to kill someone who had destroyed your comic book collection. He wanted to say, "Get off my bed! Get out of my room!"

Instead, he stood speechless for several moments, watching Parker eat, and then turned on his heel and left the room.

"Oh, and Simon," Parker called after him, "bring me another bag of Cheesios from the kitchen, wouldja?"

"Mother, can I ask you something?" said Simon. She was helping him arrange a sleeping bag on the foldout living room couch, which was to be his bed for who knows how long.

"I know what you're going to say, Simon. You don't like Parker, and you don't like sleeping on the couch. But Parker can't sleep out here because of the dust. There's nothing to be done about it. You must be polite to him."

"No. I was going to ask you if you like having Aunt Bea and Uncle Fred here."

"Why, of course! Fred's your father's brother. I love him."

"But do you *like* having them stay with us?"

"It's a little awkward and inconvenient, all of us having to go to bed at nine o'clock so you can sleep in the living room, but, well—"

"Do you like Aunt Bea?"

"Of course I do! Why shouldn't I? She can be a little, um, loud—"

"And bossy and rude."

"Simon! Lower your voice. She might hear you. You must not talk about your aunt that way."

"Why not?"

"Well, because—" His mother broke off and stared hard at him. "Simon Maxwell, I have never heard you speak this way before. You used to be so well behaved. Where are your manners? Is this Matilda's doing? What on earth has she been filling your head with? Oh, I knew I shouldn't have let you go there. I knew it! Fred was right."

"No, Mother, you're wrong. I had a wonderful time.

And I learned all about manners." He climbed into his sleeping bag. "Someday I'll tell you all about it."

His mother looked doubtful. Then she smoothed his hair and bent to kiss him. "All right, Simon. As long as you mind your manners while they're here."

"Yes, Mother."

"Get some sleep. School tomorrow. And it's a big day for you."

Simon frowned. "Why?"

"Simon! Tomorrow's your birthday! Did you forget?"

Simon's head sank back into the pillow. "My birthday. I almost forgot." He had hardly thought of it at all at Aunt Mattie's. There was an awkward pause.

"I know it's late, but would you like me to invite anyone special?" His mother wore an anxious look. Birthday parties were always a problem for Simon. He never got asked to other kids' parties, and he'd given up asking them to his.

"No," he said slowly. Then he had an idea. It popped into his mind at that instant, fully formed, like a turtle hatching from an egg. It was the solution to everything. "Wait—yes. There *is* someone I want you to ask." He sat up in bed. "Aunt Mattie and Uncle Philbert."

"Oh no, Simon," his mother answered, clearly taken aback. "We can't do that."

"Why not?"

"Well, because . . . because they live too far away. And because Aunt Bea and Uncle Fred—"

"It's not far by car," answered Simon. "Please!"

"I just don't know, Simon. I'll have to think about it. Good-night."

"Good-night," said Simon. Mrs. Maxwell left and

Simon thought about his cousin, sleeping in Simon's room on Simon's bed. "Bad-night to you, Parker." Then, remembering his training, he added, "You overinflated landlubber." He smiled. Uncle Philbert would have liked that.

Very Discombobulate

On the morning of his birthday, Simon walked into the kitchen, where his mother labored by the stove.

His father was on the phone. Simon could tell he was talking to his boss, Mr. Hackney.

"Yes, sir, I'd be happy to, sir. No problem." He saw Simon and smiled, silently mouthing the words *Good morning*.

Simon mouthed *Good morning* back to him and turned to his mother.

"And how does your corporosity seem to gashiate today?" he asked.

"Could you pass me that oven mitt?" asked his mother. "Gosh, I've burned these. Oh, good morning, Simon," she added, as if she'd just seen him. "Happy birthday. I'm afraid we're out of Rice Poppies." She glanced at the kitchen table, where Parker sat eating a large bowl of Simon's favorite cereal. Parker made a sad face and shook the empty box of Rice Poppies.

"Sorry, old boy." He smiled.

"That's okay, Mother. I'll have pizza."

That got his mother's attention. "You'll do no such thing!" she said. "I'll make you some oatmeal."

"Okay," said Simon with a sigh, adding to himself, "Very discombobulate, great congruity, dissimilarity." Suddenly, he thought of something. "Mother, did you remember to invite Aunt Mattie and Uncle Philbert?"

"Well now, Simon, I just couldn't." She glanced toward Uncle Fred and Aunt Bea and put a finger over her lips. "It wouldn't work out with, you know," she whispered, cocking her head toward the relatives. "They wouldn't get along." She handed Simon his bowl of oatmeal. He took it without a word.

Breakfast was a silent affair, because Uncle Fred was reading Mr. Maxwell's newspaper, and he needed complete quiet for this ritual.

Mr. Maxwell watched Uncle Fred from the kitchen, where he was still tied to the phone. He was fuming—but silently. Simon knew his father hated to have his newspaper pulled apart before he'd had a chance to read it, and that's just what Uncle Fred was doing. He'd even ripped out an article called "You and Your Home Equity Loan" that he apparently found interesting, leaving a gaping hole in the comics page Simon had planned to read. Simon could see his father's face grow red. His mother, meanwhile, was frantically preparing three different breakfasts for their visitors—oatmeal for Uncle Fred, more cereal and toast for Parker, and eggs and bacon for Aunt Bea.

"Good morning, Uncle Fred," said Simon.

"Mmm," grunted Uncle Fred without looking up.

"And how does your corporosity seem to gashiate?"

asked Simon, who began carrying on a little conversation with himself. "Very discombobulate? Oh, really? That's good. And it's your birthday, too? Oh, happy birthday, Simon. Thank you. No, really. Not at all."

Uncle Fred looked at him over the top of the newspaper. He frowned slightly.

"Simon, I'm surprised at you. Your father and I were

brought up to believe that children should be seen and not heard."

Simon sighed and found himself thinking wistfully of Uncle Philbert's Twenty-Four-Alarm Chili; if he had it now, he'd substitute it for the oatmeal Uncle Fred was blindly eating behind his newspaper. Give him a real surprise!

But Simon ate his oatmeal quietly. He thought back to the last time Uncle Fred and Aunt Bea had visited. He had smiled and sat with them in the living room and told them how happy he was at school, and that yes, he certainly *was* looking forward to having a chance to spend some time with Parker. And he thanked them for the "nice" stationery they gave him for Christmas ("So you can write *us* thank-you letters, pah-hah-hah!" his aunt had said with her explosive, braying laugh). And later Simon had sat at his desk and carefully written a two-page thank-you letter for the stationery. And Parker had played with Simon's favorite Christmas present, despite Simon's pleas to leave it alone, and had broken it, then laughed when Simon was upset. And Simon had covered up for Parker and told his parents he had broken it himself and then of course had gotten in trouble.

From the kitchen, he could hear Aunt Bea discussing cleaning with his mother. She was giving Mrs. Maxwell precise instructions on the right and wrong way to remove dust from rugs and curtains.

"Simon, dear," said his mother as he placed his unfinished oatmeal in the sink, "have you tidied the living room? The cleaning woman is coming soon and—there she is!" His mother hastened to answer the door. "Oh, Doris, come right in. Here, let me take your hat."

Doris was a large and frowning woman. Simon had never seen her smile, and his mother seemed to live in terror of her. Doris looked all around her as Mrs. Maxwell took her coat and hat, her gaze coming to rest on the visiting relatives.

"Large crowds still here, I see," she said with that note of disapproval in her voice. "Large crowds make lots of dirt."

"Yes, Doris."

"Lots of dirt makes lots of work for Doris."

"Yes, well, I've been tidying today, so . . ." His mother's voice trailed off. For the first time, Simon wondered if all mothers went around the house cleaning up before the cleaning lady came. Once, he'd even seen his mother scrubbing the toilet because it was "too dirty," even, apparently, for the cleaning lady to clean.

Doris went grumpily about her work, with Aunt Bea trailing behind and giving instructions, all of which Doris ignored. Mr. Maxwell came into the kitchen with his briefcase. He hadn't had time to eat breakfast or read the paper. As Mrs. Maxwell gathered up Aunt Bea and Uncle Fred's dishes, she paused to kiss him good-bye, saying cheerily, "When will you be home, dear?"

"I'll miss dinner," said Mr. Maxwell. "Mr. Hackney has asked me to work late all this week. I have no choice."

"But, George, you haven't seen Simon for two weeks, and it's his birthday today! You can't miss that. We're going to have a little party. I'm making tacos, his favorite meal."

Mr. Maxwell looked stricken. "Our biggest client is flying in from Ohio tonight. Dubble Bubble chewing gum. I'm supposed to take him to dinner and make my big presentation. You remember, 'Double, double toil and trouble.'"

Simon said nothing.

"Damn. Simon, I'm terribly sorry."

Simon stared at the ground. His father never swore. He must really be sorry. But Simon couldn't imagine a birthday party without his father.

"That's okay, Father," he said finally, without looking up. "I don't mind. Really."

Aunt Bea chose this moment to interrupt. "Oh, I'm afraid Uncle Fred can't eat tacos," she said. But Simon thought she didn't really sound afraid of anything. "Spicy foods don't agree with him. And that roughage, he can't have roughage."

This seemed as good a time as any for Simon to make his escape. He left the kitchen without saying good-bye. But instead of heading for the door—he was already late for the bus—he darted into his room, or rather, the living room. He picked up the phone and, as quietly as possible, started dialing. It rang and rang, and Simon prayed someone would answer. Finally, after about twenty rings, the phone was picked up.

"Hello?" said Simon.

"Don't want any," snapped a gruff voice.

Simon smiled.

Simple Simon

Simon dashed out the door without saying good-bye and headed for the bus stop. He had almost reached it when he heard footsteps coming quickly up behind him. Instinctively, Simon started running; if it was Peters and Shapiro, he figured, he could get to the relative safety of the bus stop before they caught him.

"Hey, Simon, wait up." It was Parker, puffing and bright red. "You're supposed to take me to the bus stop, dork."

Of course. Parker was going to have to ride Simon's bus, and Simon had been told to show him where to wait for it. His cousin gave him a rough cuff on the head, the kind of painful gesture that he often pretended was "just playing."

"Where are your manners, you dweeb."

"I'm sorry, I forgot," mumbled Simon. Though his cousin went to the same school, he was older and had classes in a different building. The two usually never saw each other at all during the day, which was fine with Simon.

As they rounded the corner, he saw he had been wrong about Peters and Shapiro. They weren't behind him. They were ahead of him—already waiting at the bus stop. Simon slowed down and prayed the bus would come soon.

"Who's your fat friend?" asked Peters. The older of the two boys, he was already a foot taller than Simon.

"Hey, Simple Simon met a pie man," snickered Shapiro, and the two boys guffawed at their wonderful joke. Simon was used to the teasing and ignored it, but he looked at Parker, expecting his cousin to respond. After all, Shapiro and Peters were big, but so was Parker. Instead, Parker flushed and turned his back on the pair. Parker had inherited his mother's red hair, and when he turned red, he really turned red. Though his back was

turned, Simon could see he had pulled out his asthma inhaler and was trying to breathe into it without anyone noticing.

Just then the bus arrived, and the two older boys shoved their way on board, followed by Simon and Parker. Simon knew enough to watch out for the legs that were always thrust into the aisle to trip him, but Parker didn't. When his cousin went sprawling onto the floor, Simon looked away, praying that Parker would not sit next to him.

He had known that Parker would make his life miserable at home. But it had never crossed his mind that Parker could add to his miseries at school this way. Yet another thing to be teased about. When the kids on the bus started chanting beneath their breath, he couldn't tell this time if they were saying "Simon, Simon" or "Pie man, pie man." Did it matter?

Toil and Trouble

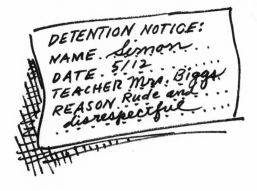

When Simon got on the bus to go home after school that day, he was filled with a calm, happy feeling. Which was really strange, considering that the reason for that feeling was a pink detention slip in his back pocket—the first detention slip of his life.

He was feeling so calm and happy that he didn't even notice that no one tried to trip him when he got on the bus. He hardly noticed when Parker sat down beside him and the kids started chanting "Pie man, pie man."

"What's with you?" asked Parker. "You look like you won the lottery or something."

"Yeah, well, I got a detention," said Simon, and he couldn't help grinning.

"Why's that so great? Are you crazy? What'd you get it for?"

Simon thought a moment. "For not taking any guff, I guess."

"Huh?"

Simon gave Parker a quick rehash of the scene with Mrs. Biggs. Simon had been daydreaming, the way he always did in math class. He was so good at math that he never needed to pay much attention, the answers just kind of came to him. He'd been thinking about Raspberry and Hero when he heard Mrs. Biggs start lighting into Jimmy Bennett. She was talking in that sarcastic way she had, making fun of Jimmy for not being able to do the problem she'd written on the board.

"So I just interrupted her—didn't even raise my hand or anything—and told her she was wrong and Jimmy was right. It's true. Jimmy had the right answer. I don't know why I did it. It just kind of came out of my mouth before I could think."

"So what happened?"

"Her jaw dropped about a mile and a half. Then she told me I was rude and disrespectful. And she sent me to the principal's office. I had to sit in the red chair in the hall. I wish you could've seen her face."

"Oh, man, I hate that red chair."

Simon didn't answer him. He was thinking of the way all the kids in his class had smiled at him, given him a thumbs-up, or even—like Jimmy—a high five when they walked past him sitting in the hall there.

But Parker's next comment wiped the dreamy smile off Simon's face and made him sit up. "Your butt is gonna be in a sling when *you* get home," he said. "Whenever I bring home a detention slip, my dad fries me."

Simon didn't have time to think about this problem, for the bus was at their stop. As the cousins headed for the steps, Simon saw Peters and Shapiro coming up in back of them. He reached a hand for the railing just as a foot hooked his ankle. Simon pitched down the steps, grabbing the railing at the last minute. But he collided heavily with Parker, knocking him out the door.

"Whoops," said Peters loudly, for the benefit of the bus driver. "Gosh, are you okay?" As soon as the doors closed behind them and the yellow bus pulled away, Peters and Shapiro began laughing. "Golly gee," they repeated, with mock sympathy, "are you poor little boys okay?"

"Let's go," said Simon urgently to Parker. They set off at a trot, but the older boys were right behind them.

"Simple Simon!" yelled Peters.

"Hey, pie man," yelled Shapiro.

"Ignore them," hissed Simon to Parker, picking up his pace. "Come on, *run*."

He broke into a run, but beside him Parker was bright red, breathing with difficulty and patting his pockets for his inhaler.

"Can't you go any faster?"

"No," gasped Parker.

Simon slowed down, grabbed Parker by the elbow, and began propelling him forward. It was useless. The older boys caught up to them.

"Don't you know it's rude to walk away when someone's talking to you?" shouted Shapiro. Simon kept going, pushing Parker along in front of him.

Suddenly, a hand caught Simon by the shoulder and spun him roughly around. It was Peters. Before Simon knew what was happening, he was on the ground, with Peters astride him, Simon's hands pinned to the ground. Peters laughed as Simon struggled to throw him off. It was no use. The older boy was much heavier, much stronger. Simon was helpless.

Shapiro looked on, smirking. Parker was nowhere to be seen.

"Get off me," said Simon angrily. Peters was so heavy on his chest, Simon could hardly breathe, and the words came out as a rasp.

"Make me." Peters laughed. "Hey, Shapiro, lookit me—I'm a cowboy." He pumped up and down on Simon's chest, pretending to ride a horse. "Lookit my horse. Giddyap, horse."

"Get off," begged Simon.

"Say 'Uncle,' little horsie," said Peters, bouncing harder.

Simon felt like his ribs were cracking. He opened his mouth to say "Uncle," but in that moment he thought of Hero. And Uncle Philbert. And with the last bit of breath in his body, he lifted his head up as high as he could and waited until Peters was grinning down at him.

"Say 'Unc—' "

Simon let fly the biggest gob of spittle he could manage.

It hit Peters square in the eye.

Peters yelped and jumped up, dabbing at his eye and making disgusted noises. He turned to Simon, full of wrath. But Simon had scrambled to his feet, and before Peters could open his mouth, Simon launched another gob of spit, beautifully aimed. This one flew a distance of several feet and hit Peters just as squarely in the other eye.

Then Simon walked up to Peters. He stuck his face into the older boy's face, the way he'd seen his aunt Mattie do to the llamas when she was preparing to chew them out good and proper.

"You," he said slowly, "are a flocculent, flea-bitten, goat-faced, son-of-a-sea-slug." Then he turned his back on him and walked deliberately away. Though he was terrified, Simon refused to hurry his steps.

A noise from behind made Simon turn. He clenched his fists, ready for anything. But the two bullies weren't chasing him—weren't even looking at him.

Shapiro was standing by Peters, pointing at him and shaking with helpless laughter.

" 'Son-of-a-sea-slug,' " he repeated, gasping for breath. "That was good, Peters. You *are* kinda goat-faced, you know. And when he got you, splat, right in the eye—"

Peters gave Shapiro a shove in the chest that landed him in the dust. Shapiro sat there, still shaking with laughter. Soon the two were scuffling and rolling in the dirt.

Simon walked on.

Parker came out from behind a lilac bush, where he had apparently been hiding the whole time.

"Hey," he said, in a different voice than Simon had heard him use before. "That was so awesome. How'd you learn to spit and cuss like that?"

Simon looked at his cousin, thinking, The jerk ditched me. Saw I was in trouble and ran off and hid. Simon tried to feel angry at Parker. But it was no good. All he could feel for him was pity.

"Oh, it's nothing," said Simon, managing at least to put a little bit of scorn into his voice. "Just some ruderies my aunt and uncle taught me."

"Your aunt—you mean *my* mother and father?" Parker was shocked. Simon had to laugh at the thought of Aunt Bea and Uncle Fred cussing.

"No, Great-aunt Mattie and Uncle Philbert. That's how they talk to the llamas. And they have a parrot with the foulest mouth in the world."

"Wow. What a great aunt and uncle."

"They're your great-aunt and great-uncle, too."

"Maybe I can go visit them someday. Naw, that would never happen. Not in a million years would my parents let me visit. I'm surprised yours did."

Simon considered Parker for a moment. Having Uncle Fred and Aunt Bea for your parents must be pretty unbearable—even worse than having them for your aunt and uncle.

"They only let me go because we had to make room for you. I mean—" Simon stopped, aware of how his words sounded. He found himself feeling sorry for Parker, not wanting to hurt his feelings. This was absurd! He loathed Parker. Didn't he?

"Yeah, well, I guess it is a pain, having me in your room."

"Kind of," he admitted.

"Listen, could you teach me to spit like that? And cuss?"

Simon thought for a moment. "All right," he said. "But I want to sleep in my own room again."

"No sweat," said Parker. "You can have the bed. I'll sleep on the floor."

"And I want my comic books back."

"All right. I'll even throw in the Spider-Man one that I just bought. Deal?"

"Deal," said Simon, laughing. He turned and punched Parker in the arm—just hard enough.

Carrot Cake and Spinach Pasta

RED FROSTING
CHOCOLATE MARBLE

"It's lovely the way the boys get on so well together, isn't it?" Aunt Bea was saying to Mrs. Maxwell. She was helping frost the cake for Simon's party. "I've always said they were more like best friends than cousins. And it must be wonderful for Simon to have his older cousin around, to look after him on the bus and so on. Someone to look up to and admire, like a big brother."

"Mmm, yes, mustn't it?" said Mrs. Maxwell brightly. As she couldn't think of anything more to say on the subject, she added, "Um, don't you think red icing for the edges?"

"No, no, dearest," said Aunt Bea a bit sadly, as if to a hopelessly stupid four-year-old. "Red food coloring contains dyes that cause hyperactivity and hives. For Parker, that is. And they are very bad for everyone in general."

"But it's Simon's favorite color."

"A pity. He must learn to like green, then."

"Yes. Green. Well, I'm sure you're right."

"Of course I am! I'm—oh, here comes the birthday boy. Get out of the kitchen, you naughty boy—not allowed to see your cake till suppertime!"

Simon laughed and hid his eyes.

"Okay," he said. "Just tell me—chocolate marble cake with red frosting, right?"

"Um, well, not exactly," said his mother with a nervous laugh.

"What do you mean?" asked Simon. "That's what you always make for my birthday! It's my favorite."

"Yes, and very bad for you, too," Aunt Bea chimed in. "No sir, today we're having carrot cake with green frosting."

"*Carrot* cake?"

"Yes, full of vitamin C. No added sugar or artificial flavors. Extremely healthful. And instead of tacos—really,

Shirley, I don't know how you can feed your family such junk food—we're having spinach pasta with whole-wheat bread and sun-dried tomatoes."

"Carrot cake? Spinach pasta?" Simon was reeling. He shot his mother a look that said, *How could you?* And she sent back a pleading look that said very clearly, *Be nice. Please.*

Simon trudged into the living room and sat glaring out the window. What was the matter with his mother and father? he wondered. Why wouldn't they stand up for him? His mother let Aunt Bea ruin his party. His father wouldn't tell the boss he needed to be home for his own son's birthday.

"How many shall I set the table for?" asked Aunt Bea in the kitchen.

"Well, let's see, three of you and two of us makes—"

"Seven," said Simon, staring out the window with a huge grin on his face.

"No, dear, I wish you wouldn't interrupt like that. Three plus two makes five—"

"Seven." Simon pointed out the window, his grin growing even bigger.

There, pulling up into the Maxwells' driveway, was Aunt Mattie's ancient black car. Uncle Philbert was in the passenger seat. The goldfish bowl was on the dashboard. Raspberry sat between Mattie and Philbert, his front feet on the dashboard, his eyes on the fish. And Runcible perched on Mattie's broad hat.

That Dreadful Woman

Simon darted out of the house and up to the car just as Mattie heaved herself out of the door.

"Aunt Mattie!" he cried, and ran into her arms. "You came! I knew you'd come."

"Mind the parrot, my dear," said Mattie, dabbing at her hair, which, as usual, was escaping from several large hairpins beneath an enormous hat decorated with fruit. She was wearing a geranium-colored dress. "Oh, blastify these hairpins. Am I late?" Runcible hopped down to Simon's shoulder and promptly bit him on the ear.

"No—ow! No, you're right on time."

"Oh, dear. I'm afraid that's because I left my watch at home. Runcible, behave yourself, you contumelious creature. Come to Mama." Runcible walked back onto Mattie's finger and then to her shoulder, where she began chewing the fruit that bedecked Mattie's hat.

From the doorway, Bea and Mrs. Maxwell watched the scene in the driveway. Mrs. Maxwell's face was a picture of dismay.

"That dreadful woman!" exclaimed Aunt Bea. "Who invited *her*?"

"Not me. I mean, not I," stammered Mrs. Maxwell, who, even in distress, strove for correct grammar.

The passenger door opened, and Uncle Philbert climbed from the car.

"Don't say hello to your great-uncle or anything," he grumped. Simon detached himself from Aunt Mattie and went over to give him a hug. "Humph. Didn't anyone ever teach you any manners?"

"Not likely," said Simon. He pulled away from his uncle, lowered his chin to his chest, and burped—or pretended to—then jabbed himself in the forehead and punched his uncle on the arm.

"Still faking it, I see," said Philbert sadly. "Boy, when are you going to learn that it's all in the throat muscle—"

"But I am getting good at interrupting," said Simon, laughing.

"Well, Simon," said Mattie, pulling a large bag out of the car, "I see that your corporosity is gashiating nicely. Here, we've got lots of presents for you. But we mustn't stand here yammering. Where are your manners? Invite us in. I'd love to see your father—haven't seen him since he was a boy. And I've never met your mother—"

"Father's not here," said Simon quickly.

"What?" Mattie's eyebrows shot up. "Missing your birthday? Must be something *awfully* important."

"It's a chewing-gum magnate from Ohio," Simon explained. "A very important client. He's taking him out to dinner tonight."

"Oh, I see. A pity. Well, then, let's get these things inside and get down to business."

The three started for the door, but just at that moment a large black limousine pulled into the driveway behind them. Simon's father climbed out of the backseat and sprinted up to them.

"Simon! We were passing by on the way to the restaurant and I convinced Mr. Hackney to stop off so I could wish you a happy birthday. We're in a terrible hurry. I've only got a second." He glanced anxiously back at the limousine and then seemed to notice Mattie and Philbert for the first time. "What's all this?"

"This, Father, is Great-aunt Mattie and Uncle Philbert. They've come for my birthday." His father looked dumbstruck. "*I* invited them."

There was a whirring sound from the limo as one of the tinted windows was lowered. Mr. Hackney stuck his head outside. He was talking on the car phone. Simon could see another man in a dark suit sitting beside him. He must be the chewing-gum magnate, the very important client from Ohio. Mr. Dubble Bubble himself.

"Make it quick, Maxwell," said Mr. Hackney. He went back to his phone and whirred the window up.

"Yes, sir," said Mr. Maxwell to the tinted window. And then to Simon: "I'm really sorry to miss your party, son." He turned to Mattie and Philbert. For a moment, Simon saw his eye take in Philbert's faded farm clothes, Mattie's fruity hat, her geranium dress, the parrot, the decrepit car. He glanced nervously toward the limo, then stuck out a hand. "Aunt Mattie, Uncle Philbert. Wonderful to see you again," he said politely. He turned back to Simon and put his hands on his son's shoulders. "Well, Simon, I want you to have a very happy—"

There was another whir.

"Hurry it *up*, Maxwell!"

Whir.

A brief silence. Then Mattie walked over to the limousine and knocked on the window. It whirred open, and Hackney's exasperated face was visible. Mattie bent over and peered around the limo with undisguised curiosity. Then she smiled sweetly, opened her mouth, and said, "Say please!"

There was a stunned silence. Simon, who recognized Runcible's voice, closed his eyes. He wasn't sure he could watch this.

"I beg your pardon?" asked Mr. Hackney in a whisper.

"Say please," said Runcible once again, in a loud, clear voice. And then she added, "Dog breath!"

Simon's father gasped and turned pale, but Aunt Mattie nodded approvingly to Hackney. "I'm sure you meant to say please, didn't you? As in '*Please* hurry it up, Mr. Maxwell.' Though I hasten to add that you don't really have dog breath."

"Maxwell, what is the meaning of this?" called Mr. Hackney, his face a dangerous plum color. Beside him, Mr. Dubble Bubble was staring in fascination as Uncle Philbert approached the car.

"I don't know, sir. I've never met this woman before in my life."

Simon couldn't believe his ears. "Father!" he said. But his father wouldn't look at him.

At that moment, Uncle Philbert stuck out his hand.

"Howdy," he said to Mr. Hackney. "I'm Uncle Philbert."

Hackney glared at Simon's father. "We're wasting time!" he hissed. Then he looked at Uncle Philbert. "How d' you do?" he muttered quickly.

"What?" said Uncle Philbert.

"I said, 'How do you do?'" Hackney repeated with an air of disbelief, as if talking to an idiot.

Simon closed his eyes again, knowing what was coming. Perhaps the ground might open up just then and swallow him, he thought. Swallow all of them.

"I heard you fine," said Uncle Philbert, whom the ground refused to swallow. "I just wanted to know, how do I do *what*? Cartwheels? Algebra? The dishes? You see, there's a different answer for—"

"Maxwell," shouted Mr. Hackney, "get these people out of our way. You've got two seconds to get in this car!"

"Yes, sir!" said Simon's father, a look of numb horror on his face. Simon felt his own sense of horror melting away. He slipped his hand into his father's and looked up at him.

"Don't go," he said. "Come to my party. Please, Dad."

Mr. Maxwell looked at Simon's solemn face and then at Mr. Hackney's purple one. Then he saw Aunt Mattie, who had reappeared beside the limo window. She was carrying something under her arm.

"Why, George Maxwell," she said. "Have you forgotten everything I taught you when you were a boy?"

Simon looked from one to the other in amazement. "Taught *him*?" he asked in surprise. "Dad, did you have un-lessons, too?"

"Un-lessons?" said Mr. Maxwell slowly. "Yes, un-lessons . . ."

"Two seconds, Maxwell."

But Mr. Maxwell was looking at Aunt Mattie. Suddenly, his expression changed. He looked like someone who has finally remembered his dream of the night before. A smile crept over his face, and he looked down at Simon. "Un-lessons," he repeated.

"Well," said Hackney. "I'm waiting for an answer."

"No, no," said Mr. Maxwell distractedly, not even looking at Hackney. "No, I'm not coming."

"What? *What?* Have you lost your mind?"

"No, Mr. Hackney. I haven't lost my mind. I'm going to stay here and go to my son's birthday party. And I would like to add, sir"—here, he bent over in order to stare straight into Hackney's face, and Simon tightened his grip on his father's arm—"I would like to add that I have always felt that you, Mr. Hackney, are a bottom-feeding, talent-free, money-grubber. Sir."

Mr. Hackney gasped. "Maxwell," he hissed, "I'll give you exactly one second to apologize for that nonsense and get in this car or else—"

"Or else what?" asked Uncle Philbert. "Or else you'll give him two seconds?"

"I've got it!" said Mattie.

"What?" said the startled Hackney.

"The solution to the goldfish problem. You see, life is so boring for goldfish." She produced the fishbowl with a flourish. "But you've got this big car with a great view. All this tinted glass! And that place there"—she pointed to the liquor bar between the front and back seats—"that's a perfect spot for the bowl. I was going to give these fish to Simon for his birthday, but this is a much

110

better home for them. Here you go. Don't bother to say thank you, really. Just remember to feed them twice a day."

Mr. Hackney's jaw dropped. Mattie thrust the bowl through the window and onto the liquor bar. The cat, Raspberry, having escaped from Mattie's car, chose that exact moment to make his move on the fish. He leaped through the open window, landing in Mr. Hackney's lap. Mr. Hackney yelped and dropped his car phone. The

phone landed in the goldfish bowl, the goldfish bowl landed—upside down—in Mr. Hackney's lap, and the fish themselves landed on the car seat.

"Maxwell!" sputtered Hackney. "This is outrageous!" He turned to the client beside him. "I'm terribly, *terribly* sorry, sir." And then to Simon's father again: "Apologize instantly or you're fired."

"I beg to differ," said Mr. Dubble Bubble, climbing out of his side of the car and handing Raspberry over to Mattie. "It is you, Mr. Hackney, who are fired. Where I come from, we treat our employees with more respect than that."

Mr. Hackney looked amazed. The color drained from his face.

"But what about Dubble Bubble gum? You can't mean this. What about our dinner?"

Simon spoke up. "I'm sure Mother can set another place for dinner. You're welcome to eat with us."

Mr. Dubble Bubble looked pleased. "I'd be honored to join your birthday party." He glanced at Hackney. "I won't be needing your services anymore, Mr. Hackney."

Mr. Hackney opened and shut his mouth a few times—something like a goldfish, thought Simon. Then he turned and ordered the limousine driver to leave.

"You are a fool, Maxwell," called Hackney.

"And you, sir," said Philbert, opening the car door, "are sitting on a goldfish." He plucked the fish and the bowl from the backseat. Hackney slammed the door, and the limo sped out the driveway.

Uncle Philbert waved good-bye to the car.

"Have a nice day," he said.

Happy Birthday

The birthday party was probably the strangest one of Simon's short life.

At first, Mr. Maxwell sat in a kind of stupor while Aunt Bea asked him over and over, "Did you quit? Were you fired?" Then she would turn to Uncle Fred and whisper, "He's been fired. It's all that dreadful woman's fault."

But Mr. Maxwell just shook his head. "I don't know. Did I? Was I?"

Mr. Dubble Bubble gave a great laugh and clapped Simon's father on the back. "No, you weren't fired. Hackney didn't have the guts. Even after you called him a—what was it you called him?"

"A talent-free, bottom-feeding money-grubber," said Philbert happily.

"Ha! That's a good one. Gotta remember that one," said Mr. Dubble Bubble with great satisfaction.

"What do you mean, he didn't have the guts to fire me?" asked Mr. Maxwell, seeming to wake up.

"He didn't. He knows how good you are," said Mr. Dubble Bubble. "He showed me your ad copy—'Double, double toil and trouble.' Ha! Very clever! He didn't dare lose you. You are his best writer, Mr. Maxwell. He told me so himself. Oh, he may not have treated you that way. He was going to work you to the bone, is my guess. He must have been very sure you'd never quit."

Mr. Maxwell was silent for a long moment. "Well," he said, and a grin spread across his face, "I guess he's going to find out he was wrong."

"Good for you!" said the bubble-gum magnate. "I hope you and I—"

But Simon couldn't hear what else he said, because at that moment Aunt Mattie spoke up to point out that the idea of a *birthday party* was to open *presents*, thank you very much, and not just for grown-ups to blab on and on about *business*.

Simon made a great show of loving all his presents, when what he was really loving was that his father was here to share them with him. And Aunt Mattie and Uncle Philbert. He even smiled and thanked Aunt Bea for her present—two goldfish in a plastic bag. She seemed to have forgotten that she had given Simon goldfish for his last birthday.

"That makes six," he said, adding them to the bowl with Mattie's fish. "I promise to feed them twice a day and take them for rides in the car so they don't get bored." And he exchanged a secret wink with Aunt Mattie.

From Uncle Philbert, there was a bone-handled jack-knife with a mumblety-peg blade. Philbert had also brought a huge batch of special Seventy-Three-Alarm

Chili—"for dessert." And Mattie had brought a chocolate marble cake, with red frosting. "I thought you might need an extra," she explained to Mrs. Maxwell.

"Thank you," Simon's mother said. Her cheeks were bright pink. She glanced quickly at Fred and Bea before adding, "It's Simon's favorite, you know."

When they sat down to eat, Aunt Bea and Uncle Fred refused to touch the chili, of course. They just said, "We couldn't possibly consider eating food like that." Instead, they ate spinach pasta.

When it came Simon's turn, he said, "Thank you for making the pasta, Aunt Bea, but I think I'll try this chili." Bea and Fred exchanged a glance that said, *How rude!* But Simon pretended not to see it.

When it came time for dessert, Mrs. Maxwell brought out the carrot cake, only to be greeted with a cry from Mr. Dubble Bubble. "Carrot cake! Why eat carrot cake when you have a perfectly beautiful marble cake with red frosting?"

And because he was a guest, no one could object. So they all ate marble cake for dessert. All except Aunt Bea and Uncle Fred, who insisted that they—and Parker—eat the carrot cake.

Then Simon made a wish and blew out the candles. There was a pause. Simon looked at his father. He wanted to tell him that he'd already gotten his wish.

"Dad, I—" began Simon.

"Well, George," said Uncle Fred, clearing his throat loudly, "what are you going to do about a job now?"

"What?" said Mr. Maxwell.

"Um, Dad, could I—" said Simon.

"Simon, dear, you're interrupting," said Aunt Bea patiently. "Besides, you know you shouldn't speak before being spoken to."

Parker spoke for the first time.

"He was not interrupting," he said hotly. "*You* were."

There was a stunned silence all around.

"Perhaps now would be the time for me to give you your last present, Simon," said Aunt Mattie quickly. She rose from the table. "It's in the car. I'll just go get it."

As she left, Simon turned to his father and said, "Dad, I wanted to tell you that I was really proud of what you did today."

"Simon, how can you say that?" said Uncle Fred sternly. "Your father just lost his job."

"Yes," added Aunt Bea. "Six months from now, you may all be in the poorhouse. And all because of that woman."

"Just a moment," said Mr. Maxwell. " 'That woman' happens to be my aunt—and a very fine woman. And it wasn't her fault I lost my job. Heck, if I finally have the guts to stand up to Hackney—something I should have done years ago—I don't want to go handing the credit out to other people."

"Yeah, Dad, you were great," said Simon.

"I can't believe what I'm hearing," said Aunt Bea. "You're defending that woman? After she gets you fired? And she has clearly turned your son into a rude, selfish little beast. He used to be such a nice boy."

"See here, Bea—" began Simon's mother, and her voice had a ring of iron to it that Simon had never heard before.

But Mr. Dubble Bubble interrupted. "George is working for me," he said. "Isn't that right? That is, if you want to."

Mr. Maxwell smiled. "I think I'm going to go into business for myself. Be my own boss. And Dubble Bubble gum will be my first client."

Just then, Mattie returned to the dining room. In her arms was the cat Raspberry, who took one look at Simon and bounded straight into his lap. He put his paws on Simon's chest, stuck his nose into Simon's face, and purred loudly.

"Listen to that cat," said Philbert. "Purring like a pastry."

"Happy birthday, Simon," said Aunt Mattie. "Poor Raspberry was pining away for you. He simply *insisted* on coming to live with you."

Uncle Fred and Aunt Bea gasped at the same time.

"Oh, no. No, no, no. No, I'm afraid this won't do," said Bea. "We can't have cats in the house. Absolutely out of the question."

"Parker's allergies," explained Uncle Fred patiently.

"Not to mention the fleas and cat hair and, well, diseases and things," said Aunt Bea. "The cleaning lady—Doris—you know she'd have a conniption fit."

Mrs. Maxwell stood up. "Well, let her have a fit. There are other cleaning ladies out there. Besides, who needs a cleaning lady? I think he's a lovely cat."

"Are you saying that you're *keeping* the cat?" asked Aunt Bea, unable to believe her ears.

Mrs. Maxwell looked at Mr. Maxwell. They both looked at Simon. Simon buried his head in Raspberry's warm fur.

"Yes. We're keeping the cat."

This time, Simon broke the silence.

He burped.

It was a long, satisfying, and genuine burp—just the way Uncle Philbert had taught him. Then he jabbed himself in the forehead, jumped up, and ran around the table, poking everyone in the arm. Mattie and Philbert tried to explain the game, but suddenly Runcible let

loose a terrific imitation burp, and then Mr. Dubble Bubble burped, and then Parker did a pretend burp. Suddenly, the whole table—except, of course, Aunt Bea and Uncle Fred—was convulsed in laughter, everyone punching one another in the arm, stabbing themselves in the forehead, arguing over who did what first, gasping for breath, a parrot fluttering here, a cat leaping there.

Aunt Bea and Uncle Fred stood up and surveyed the amazing, ridiculous scene.

"Perhaps we'd better be leaving," said Uncle Fred, who could hardly be heard above the noise. Uncle Philbert and Mr. Maxwell had begun an armpit duet of "Happy Birthday."

"Yes, yes, perhaps you should," said Mrs. Maxwell, trying unsuccessfully to stop giggling. She turned to Uncle Philbert. "You must teach me how you do that."

Simon lay in bed that night thinking about the extraordinary day he'd had, from the battle with Mrs. Biggs, the fight with the bullies, and the amazing birthday party, to the departure of his relatives. He'd been surprisingly sorry to see Parker leave, and asked him where he thought they'd go.

"Well," said Parker with a sly smile, "Aunt Mattie has asked me to stay with her."

"No!" said Simon. "Your parents will never agree. I thought they said you were all going to some motel for the week."

"Yes," said Parker with an even slier smile. "But I plan to develop a wicked allergy to the motel carpet." He gave a little fake cough and rubbed his eyes till they were bright red. "Works every time."

Saying good-bye to Aunt Mattie and Uncle Philbert had been even odder.

Mr. Maxwell shook hands with Uncle Philbert through the car window.

"I'm going to teach Simon how to whittle with that knife," he said. "It's a great way to pass the time. And I remember this game called mumblety-something you once taught me. It's all coming back to me."

Mrs. Maxwell was saying good-bye to Aunt Mattie. "How does that go again?" she asked through the window.

"Mangy, mucculent misfit," repeated Aunt Mattie slowly.

"That's good," said Mrs. Maxwell. "I'll remember that."

Simon produced a box from under his arm and presented it to Aunt Mattie.

"It's a present for Hero," he explained.

Mattie peeked inside. It was the rest of Aunt Bea's carrot cake.

"Goodness, he'll love it!" she exclaimed. "What a thoughtful lad you are. You know, I swear that horse misses you. I tried to bring him today, but he wouldn't fit in the car."

"Maybe Simon will have a chance to visit again," said Mr. Maxwell.

"Maybe we all will," said Mrs. Maxwell. Then, remembering it was rude to invite yourself to someone else's house, she added, "If you'll have us, of course."

Mattie seemed to be considering this idea. "Do you play tennis?" she asked.

"Oh, I'm afraid not," said Mrs. Maxwell.

"Good. In that case, you're always welcome."

There was a knock on Simon's door, and his father came in and sat on the bed.

"Good-night, son."

"Good-night, Dad."

"What happened to 'Father'?"

"I just decided I like 'Dad' better. Do you mind?"

His father considered it. "I could learn to like it," he said. Then he noticed the pink detention slip on Simon's desk. "What's this?"

"I've been meaning to tell you about it, but, well, it's sort of a long story."

"Try me," said his father, with a rueful look. "As of now, I have all the time in the world."

So Simon told him the story of the run-in with Mrs. Biggs and the trip to the principal's office. "I guess you could say I got in trouble with my boss," he concluded, with a nervous glance at his father.

Mr. Maxwell gazed out the window for a long moment. He was trying to look severe.

"No more Mr. Nice Guy, huh?" he said at last.

"I guess not," said Simon.

"Well, son"—and a big grin split Mr. Maxwell's face, despite his best efforts—"I guess that makes two of us."

Simon laughed, and so did Mr. Maxwell. But then Simon stopped. He fixed his father with a stern look.

"It depends, of course," he said. "What exactly did you mean by *nice*?"